THE TROLL BRIDE

A MONSTERLY YOURS ROMANCE

S.J. SANDERS

©2019 by Samantha J. Sanders
All rights reserved.

No part of this book may be reproduced or transmitted in any form or by any means, electronic or mechanical, including photocopying, recording, or by any information storage and retrieval system, without explicit permission granted in writing from the author.

This book is a work of fiction intended for adult audiences only.

Editor: LY Publishing

Cover Art: Sam Griffin

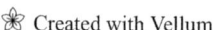 Created with Vellum

CHAPTER 1

KATE

"The fae mean us no harm. They are higher beings, ones of goodness and light..." The earnest woman on the TV is rattling on, but I'm no longer paying attention. Ever since the fae intruded on our world weeks ago, life hasn't been the same.

The morning talk show *The Fae Among Us* has been a popular outlet for people to vent their concerns or, in the case of this woman, to encourage the rest of us to see the fae as our benevolent overlords.

It never ceases to surprise me just how many people don't give the fae their due respect, like this nutcase. A smart person would recognize that the fae are powerful creatures with the potential for good, but they can just as easily embrace chaos and terror. In some cases, it's more the latter than the former.

The world of the fae isn't a G-rated construct as imagined by Disney. No, if there's any truth behind the fae of lore, their world is deadly and unkind to the ignorant. With its strict hierarchy, I imagine it isn't all too kind to its own people, either. So when the fae introduced themselves to the human world, my first impulse was to feel suspicious. What could they possibly want from our world?

Not long ago, I was comfortable in my own little world believing that the fae, monsters, and things that go bump in the night lived solely in the realm of imagination. I admit I'm a fantasy nerd to the nth degree, but imagination and reality are two different things.

It's not like I haven't imagined what it would be like. Would it be high fantasy like the world of Tolkien? I've read all his books several times and even dragged Sammi with me to see all the *Lord of the Rings* and *Hobbit* movies, because hey, no one wants to go alone. Or would it be like the numerous worlds from tabletop and roleplaying games like Magic the Gathering or Dungeons & Dragons?

I would never admit that it was all a platform to explore my fascination with what's classically labeled as "monsters." Boukie's father, Alex, was so large and imposing that he was an exceptional stand-in for my fantasies. It didn't hurt that he played that role to a T whenever he got the chance at every fair, festival, and convention we could attend. The two of us met at the local Renaissance Faire while I lived in Seattle for a short time. He was parading around as a troll dungeon master, of all things. It was love at first sight. We had problems, not the least of which was his incarceration, but he was a lot of fun when it came to our shared passions. He'd even been considering auditioning at the Castle of Muskogee in Oklahoma.

Unfortunately, that never happened. His past caught up with him and landed him in prison. He'd participated in a robbery some years prior, and a security guard had died. He hadn't shot the guy, but robbing banks still didn't sit well with the federal government. It had taken them a while to identify him, but when it happened, Alex had felt relieved that the whole thing was finally over.

After that disaster, I made the decision to come back home and found out later that I was pregnant. Through a few letters, we agreed that it would be best for Boukie if we made a clean break. Oddly enough, it was his idea. He was facing twenty-five years in prison and wanted a better man in his daughter's life. I'd promised him that I wouldn't settle for just anyone for our baby—preferably a guy who could play a half-decent troll. Alex was funny like that. Not that he had much to worry about. He was as close to a troll as I could get.

I'm not entirely sure if I have the nerve to jump a troll, even if the opportunity arises. There's something scary about actually being presented with your fantasy in the flesh.

It's not like I'm a single woman without responsibilities and obligations. I'm a mom, which means I have to do what's best for the little body trusting me not to screw up. Not that my little one wouldn't try the patience of a saint. Boyfriends never lasted long, often with the excuse that they just aren't ready to be a father to a wild toddler who requires extra attention.

As far as I'm concerned, they can go get forked. At six years old, Boukie is hell on wheels, but she's my unholy terror. Her full name is Rebecca, but Sammi started calling my little girl Boukie as a toddler and it stuck. Truthfully, it fits her better. She is not a refined Rebecca; she's a snarling, excitable mass of energy.

The phone rings as a saner person begins talking on the TV program. A middle-aged lady with a string of letters after her name cautions everyone to not overreact but also warns people not to underestimate the beings sharing our world with us once more. I nod my head in approval and lean over to check the caller ID while Boukie tries to take advantage of my momentary distraction to wiggle free from between my legs.

This is our daily routine. She tries to escape, and I attempt to hold her writhing little body still as I gently pull the brush through her mop of tangled hair. No matter how gentle I try to be, she hollers as if I'm torturing her, and that's after a liberal spritz of detangling spray. I'm starting to suspect whoever makes this stuff is either lying their ass off or doesn't know what they're talking about. It hasn't helped yet with the mass of knots she wakes up with every morning.

I wouldn't normally try and multitask while brushing Boukie's hair, but the caller ID says it's Lucy. I can't not answer the phone. She's been a surrogate mother to me ever since Sammi brought me home one day for dinner and Lucy adopted me into her brood. There isn't anything I wouldn't do for my adoptive family.

When Sammi disappeared during a blizzard in the mountains, we were all devastated. Honestly, I had a hard time believing it. Sammi is the least outdoorsy person I've ever met. The last thing she would think as 'romantic' is a weekend in the mountains, much less in the middle of winter. Still, Lucy and I keep in touch every Sunday like clockwork. Neither of us dare mention that it's possible Sammi won't be coming back. Instead, we talk about what we're going to do when she gets home and chat about what we've been up to lately. Anything to keep our spirits up.

Lucy also babysits Boukie while I'm at work, so a missed call for an emergency could leave me high and dry for a sitter. It's always best to find out early—and it's *early* right now. My shift doesn't start at the coffee shop until one, so I'm almost certain she's calling because she is either sick or something came up.

The café is a crappy job but between my wages and tips, I keep us taken care of. But I can't afford to lose a day of work. I mentally cross my fingers as I answer the phone, propping it between my cheek and shoulder.

"Hello, Lucy. How are you doing today?" I chirp pleasantly, tightening my legs around my little monster as she once again nearly escapes, and run the brush through Boukie's hair once again.

"Kate, come over now! Sammi's home!" Lucy's excited voice warbles over the phone line.

My hand tightens in surprise around the length of Boukie's hair, making my little girl squeak.

"Mommy!"

"Sorry, baby," I whisper.

I drag the brush through one more time as I gather the mess into a ponytail and secure it with a band before I can give Lucy my full attention.

"What? When did she get home?"

"Yesterday. She… arrived with some very large gray men." She pauses and I can barely hear Jake talking in the background. "Sorry. Jake says they're not men. They're orcs."

"Orcs, huh," I say. "I thought Tolkien made those up."

While there is some source material that may have been the inspiration behind Tolkien's orcs, I never suspected that orcs would be among the races now mingling with humans. Color me surprised.

"I have no idea about these types of things," Lucy says with a sigh. "I just know what I know. They're big gray fellows, and there's a bright green one who doesn't look like them—yes, thank you, Jake. He's a troll, apparently, and they all brought Sammi home."

A troll? That has to be a coincidence.

"And she's okay?" I ask slowly. Orcs and trolls willingly returning a human strikes me as unusual when compared to most fantasy lore. Then again, what isn't unusual these days?

I'm trying to not even think too much about the troll. Despite my fascination with them, trolls are almost uniformly depicted as foul brutes. There's no way of knowing how much is exaggerated

—or if they're worse. What in the world is Sammi doing running around with orcs and trolls?

"She's fine, dear. In fact, she's never been happier from what I can tell. It seems Travis has been lying through his teeth the entire time. He abandoned her alone in the mountains. She was rescued by her... uh... husband," Lucy says, her voice trembling. She sounds uncertain of exactly what to think about the entire situation and I can't say that I blame her.

My mouth drops open and I set the hairbrush down beside me.

"That dirtbag!" I exclaim, horrified that Travis had done something so rotten. But why am I surprised? I never could stand the bastard. Only then does the other part of what she said filter into my brain.

"Wait... She married an orc?" I don't even try to hide how completely bewildered this whole thing has me.

I jump up to my feet to hunt for my car keys, whipping around the living room like a tornado.

"Don't let them go anywhere. I'm on my way."

∽

Cavek

I don't want to admit it, but I am jealous of Orgath. Jealous of an orc of all beings!

I shake my head at my own foolishness. I have nothing against orcs, and I've come to admire them in the weeks I've been in their company. They possess such pride and fortitude that one would never guess they are likely the most abused species in all of Ov'Gorg by the elves.

The elves make it their business to interfere with orcs in ways that aren't in the best interests of their massive cousins. They're seen as cannon fodder whenever the kingdoms get into some skirmish or another. I never would have thought that an orc would have anything I would envy. But when I look at Sammi, the human wife of the orc chieftain, I feel it.

It doesn't help that my brief contact with human females has been… discouraging. As we moved through the city, more than one female gazed at me with lust in her eyes. I am used to that. Elves encourage the idea that trolls are ugly, hideous creatures, but females seem almost as drawn to us as they are to the fae folk, though for completely different reasons. I feel discouraged because I don't see even a spark of my potential bloodbond in any of them as I strolled by.

Unlike orcs, who possess little magic, trolls, elves, dragons, merfolk, and other magical beings can sense our bloodbond when we come across that person. It is our souls singing to one another, as my mother once described it in her obnoxiously romantic way. She actually sang, off-key, about it when trying to convince me to meet with a line-up of females she'd arranged. I shudder at the memory. That it had been in front of many of my peers made it one of the most embarrassing experiences of my life.

I had hoped that by accompanying Orgath and Sammi back to Ov'Ge that, within minutes, I would catch sight of a female meant for me. Not only would I get a mate, I would get my mother off my back. Everyone wins. I left Ov'Gorg thinking that this plan was foolproof.

Fate has a way of setting beings together. I was surely meant to have joined in company with Orgath and aided in his fight for his place as chieftain because it would lead me to my own mate. A seer, whom my mother had hired in her more recent attempts to locate my mate on my thirtieth natal day, had once implied as much.

So far, my luck has been dismal.

That is why I find myself sitting on the steps, sharpening my blades rather than being in bed with a mate. Orgath is a lucky bastard. I suppose I could be inside mingling with the others. The three other orcs who accompanied us are lurking in the kitchen, no doubt salivating as they wait for Sammi's mother, Lucy, to finish preparing the morning meal. Delicious smells waft my way from that direction.

I sheathe my blades again and decide to go check on the status of the food when a small transport vehicle—a car, if I remember correctly—stops in front of the house. It is a vivid red and looks like it's seen a great many years if the peeling paint and rust spots are anything to go by.

I cock my head with curiosity. Who would be arriving this early? A young woman jumps out of the vehicle, a messy braid of dark hair trailing past her shoulders. Instead of approaching the house, she turns to the rear of her vehicle, opens one of its doors, and leans down, disappearing from my sight. When she reappears, she is holding the tiny hand of a little human child.

My heart stirs as they approach, and the warm scent of her makes me feel dizzy. A humming sound fills my ears, fluctuating in pitch as it fills the air between us. It lasts for only a moment but everything within me stills for a time.

I know immediately that she doesn't experience the same thing I do. Or at least not the same way I experience it as a troll. It is clear, however, that she feels... something. Her gait slows and she furrows her brow as she looks at me. But rather than stop and speak to me, she pushes past and into the house, shouting for Lucy. The sound of her voice becomes the living flame that draws upon my very being, and I find myself following just behind her, unable to resist what draws me to this female.

I am aware of little as she releases her child to wander freely in the house. I don't hear the words of greeting she exchanges with Lucy. I barely notice that I am trailing behind her as she makes her way down the hall after her daughter, nor do I comprehend the words she exchanges with Sammi. I hear her name, Kate, upon Sammi's lips, and that is the only thing important enough to pull my attention away from my female.

My mate.

She is strange and small, oddly pale despite all that dark hair, and her eyes are an interesting color somewhere between brown and green. Yet to me, she is the most perfect female to have ever been born. My whole world has narrowed down to this one female, who is meant for me.

Even if she doesn't yet know it.

∼

Kate

One of them is following me around. It's a little unsettling, on one hand, but on the other he's strangely attractive. *This* is the troll? He's large and thick with muscle, although nowhere near as huge as the male orcs hovering around Lucy as she cooks, but he's prettier than I would have imagined a troll to be. He's emerald green with small bumps raised along his cheekbones and the sides of his neck and arms.

The perverse side of me that likes to forget that I'm a single mother wonders if he'd object if I looked to see if the bumps showed up anywhere else on his body. His features are larger than those of a human, from his face to his large clawed hands. His onyx black lips and sharp teeth, along with his predatory eyes and broad nose, seem most troll-ish, as do the tiny bony studs just above his eyebrows, but the long mass of luxurious lavender hair pulled back with a single leather thong is completely unexpected.

Boukie, having run off to play again after smothering Sammi with love, is watching his hair with a curiosity that concerns me.

She's never expressed any interest in the guys I've dated over the years. But she seems fascinated with this guy, who appears to be doing an excellent impression of my shadow. What is with him?

He doesn't say a word; he just hovers behind me with an intense expression that I can't make heads or tails of. It's starting to give me the creeps when, to my surprise, Boukie reaches out and grabs his hand. The troll glances down at her, at first startled but the expression softens into a captivated smile as she stares up at him with a puckish grin.

"Can I braid your hair after breakfast?" she asks him. Cavek blinks down at her and a slow grin spread on his face, baring all his sharp teeth. I worry that it is going to scare my little girl, but she again surprises me when she begins jumping up and down and clapping her hands when he nods his head.

"All right! Let's go eat. My belly is starving to death! Hurry!" she says and runs at full speed toward the dining room.

I laugh at the panic that flashes over his face.

"She's not really starving. Boukie just loves to exaggerate everything," I assure him.

His obvious relief makes me laugh all over again. Boukie seems to have won him over, but I don't realize how much until he sits down on the other side of her and proceeds to put small portions on her plate of whatever she points at. He even manages to get her to eat all of her eggs. Anyone at the table who isn't shocked at that has never had to argue with a stubborn child who refuses to eat all their eggs.

Despite the unusual company, I find myself living my dream. Cavek is an entertaining storyteller and I'm completely captivated as he talks about the troll kingdom in the depths of their forest territory. It's almost like I'm there. All that's missing is a leaky tavern and the appropriate clothes and gear, and I would be in heaven. The morning passes far too quickly, and my real life rudely intrudes.

With a sigh, I drop a kiss on my daughter's head as she plays with Cavek's long hair, twisting clumps of it into wild, sloppy braids. Beside her is a pile of rubber bands supplied by Lucy.

"You be good for Nana Lucy," I remind her.

"Yes, Mommy," my imp says.

Cavek turns his head and frowns at me.

"You are leaving?" There is a note of disapproval to the question that strikes me the wrong way.

"Yes, I can't just sit around all day. I have to work so I can afford small luxuries like food, clothes, and shelter. Lucy watches her for me. I'll be back for Boukie in a few hours," I say as I pull my shoes back on.

A warm, textured hand wraps around my wrist, startling me, and I turn to stare into Cavek's brilliant amethyst eyes. How did I not notice he had such vivid purple eyes? The remorse etched into his face surprises me even more.

"My apologies, Kate. I didn't mean to imply that it is wrong of you. It just caught me by surprise. Among trolls, one parent usually stays with the children at all times. Sometimes they trade the chore if they own a business together. In cases where a mate is absent or has died, our kingdom provides for them. Since you are alone, I assumed that you were likewise taken care of in some way. Please don't take it as criticism of you and your devotion to little Boukie."

He's so earnest that I can feel my heart melting, the resentment and anger long forgotten.

Gods, he is cute.

"No harm done," I say, unable to keep the smile from my face as I rush out the door before I say or do something else that's stupid.

CHAPTER 2

KATE

*L*arge, rough hands caress my breasts and stroke down my belly as soft, full lips kiss my shoulder. With a shiver, I can feel the damp heat gathering between my legs. I've never been so turned on in my life. I arch my hips, begging those fingers to go just a little lower. When they finally make contact, my body sings with pleasure. There's a strange graze of hard, curved nails every now and then which is peculiar, but I'm distracted by the wonderful things those talented fingers are doing to my body.

My lover flicks my clit, pinching it as a knuckle pushes into the wet folds. I groan and will myself to open my eyes despite the electric sensations shooting through me. I look and meet deep amethyst eyes and brilliant green skin.

Startled, I jerk away even as my body careens over the edge.

I snap forward with a yelp and sit up in bed. My heart hammers in my chest as I blink and look around me. I'm alone. There's no seven-foot troll anywhere in my bedroom, much less sharing my bed. I flop back down onto my sweat-soaked sheets, my thighs slick with my orgasm.

It was only a dream. I don't know if I'm disappointed or not.

I grab my phone to check the time. Five fifteen in the morning. I might as well get up, because I'm on the opening shift today.

I manage to tumble out of bed right-side up and walk across my bedroom without stubbing my toe on one of Boukie's random toys lying on the floor or otherwise killing myself. Boukie has her own room but for some reason still insists on playing in my room as well. She's pretty much taken over our entire apartment if I'm perfectly honest with myself.

After a fast shower and a twelve-ounce cup of coffee courtesy of my Keurig, the current love of my life, I feel somewhat human. Just in time to wake Boukie. With a second cup of coffee in my hand, I go into her room thoroughly decorated in princess pink and turn the light on. Pictures of unicorns, dragons, and all manner of creatures decorate her walls. She even has her own princess gown and tiara from Halloween. Truthfully, it looks like something vomited Barbie princess everywhere.

I reach down and give my baby's shoulder a gentle shake.

"Wake up, Boukie-boo. Time to get ready for kindergarten."

The little lump under the blanket scrunches up in a tight, stubborn ball.

"No," the ball of blankets mumbles petulantly.

"Yes, come on. Mommy has to work today, so you need to get up. Let's go. Nana Lucy will be picking you up from school, and you get to hang out with her until I get off work."

Signs of life manifest as Boukie pulls the blanket down and squints up at me.

"I get to see Cavek?"

I frown down at my little monster's hopeful face. I'm not sure I'm comfortable with how quickly she's taken to the troll.

"Yes," I say slowly. "You probably will."

She scrambles out of bed with a squeal, pulling off her night gown as she goes. I'm mildly impressed. Okay, maybe her fascination with Cavek won't be a bad thing after all if it gets her moving this quickly in the morning. It usually takes me twenty minutes of cajoling and damn near threatening to get her out of bed.

"Yay! Gonna see Cavek and Nana Lucy and Auntie Sammi, and all the ories," she squeaks excitedly.

"Orcs," I correct her as I wrangle her into a clean dress.

Fifteen minutes later, she has her hair neatly brushed and is waiting patiently for her cereal, her little feet pumping merrily under the table as she sings quietly to herself. I cut bananas on top of her cereal and raise a suspicious eyebrow at her as I set her bowl in front of her.

"Okay, who are you and what did you do with my Boukie?"

"Mommy, it's me!"

"Can't be," I say playfully, making Boukie giggle harder.

"It is, it is," she insists between giggles.

I sigh loudly. "Well, if you say so. I guess I'll have to keep this well-behaved little girl."

I lean down to give her a loud smacking kiss and blow a raspberry on her cheek, making her squeal.

"Eat, girl child," I say in my dungeon master voice.

Leaving Boukie to shovel cereal in her mouth, I step back into the bathroom to finish getting ready for work. It takes little time to pull on my uniform and twist my hair into its customary braid. I finish by applying my favorite dusty rose lipstick and back away from the mirror to take a better look at myself. The pink-and-brown-striped coffee shop uniform is hideous, but I suppose I wear it well enough. I can't help but think the entire ensemble screams 'desperate single mom willing to work for scraps.'

I grimace. Normally I don't care that I make just above

minimum wage slinging coffees for strangers. I make enough to cover basic bills for our little apartment and if I hustle, I can make enough in tips to afford a few indulgences. No, the problem is that last week was my twenty-ninth birthday. I'm almost thirty and no closer to doing anything I'm passionate about.

It has been suggested more than once that I take out student loans and go back to school, but for what? To find a "practical career" so that I can be in debt up to my eyebrows and still feel unsatisfied? Not that I know what I want to do. Everything has revolved around raising my baby and struggling to get by as a single parent for so long that I'm not sure exactly what I feel passionate about anymore.

What do I want?

An unbidden image of Cavek rises in my mind's eye. I shake my head. Yeah, that doesn't exactly help my situation any. It's hard enough finding a great guy who wants an instant family. Every time I get with a guy who has his shit together, he takes one look at Boukie and runs the other way. Somehow, I can't imagine a troll is going to be any more interested in raising another's child.

With ruthless determination, I push aside my fascination with Cavek. I can't allow myself to dwell on a guy out of my reach, and one that I'm not entirely convinced would be good for Boukie in the long run. At best, he and I can probably have some fun and then say goodbye when he leaves with Orgath and Sammi.

Straightening the hem on my shirt, I emerge from the bathroom and am greeted by my smiling little imp already wearing her jacket and sneakers.

"Imma ready to go, Mommy," she says with pride. "I got my shoes on by myself and everything."

"Yes, I see, baby," I reply with a smile.

She leans into me, hugging my arm as she slips her hand into mine. My heart fills. Boukie is worth everything; I have no regrets.

"What shall we sing on our way to school today, monster?"

She thinks about it for a minute, but her choice is the same as always.

"I wanna sing 'Got You Babe!'"

All it took was one time hearing Sonny and Cher belting out "I Got You Babe" on an oldies station when she was three and she was hooked.

"Sounds good to me," I say as we step out the door. She beams up at me as I lock the door behind us.

"They say we're young and we don't know we won't find out until we grow... Well, I don't know if all that's true, 'cause you got me, and baby I got you..."

"Babe!" Boukie sings at the top of her lungs with me. "I got you babe!"

∿

Cavek

As I sit with Boukie, I am impatient to see Kate again. More than once, I find myself counting the hours until she arrives to fetch her daughter. I try not to show my interest too much around the others.

Sammi has been giving me strangely hostile looks since yesterday. I am not sure why, but I suspect it has to do with Kate. Does she disapprove of my interest in her friend? That would hardly seem fair, given that she herself is mated to an orc. I considered asking Orgath, but the moment I even say Kate's name he gives me a foreboding look that effectively silences me. Considering that I'm not cowed by anyone, that's an achievement.

I'm not afraid of him, exactly, but I like breathing easy and so it seems to be in my best interest to not aggravate him.

Although I miss my female, Boukie is endless entertainment. She reminds me a little of a young troll with all her energy and bright personality. She'd arrived earlier that afternoon when Lucy picked her up from the educational place they call a school. She'd thrown a small bag on a chair and spent an hour showing me how well she has learned to write her human lettering in something called homework. The concept baffles me, but I enjoy watching her form the shaky, scrawled letters. She demonstrates each one and sternly has me follow suit.

We're sitting side-by-side as she supervises my writing when Lucy places two plates on the table. A sweet and fishy smell wafts up from two paste-laden breads.

"What is this?" I ask, breathing in the delicious aroma. Trolls live in deep forests where rivers often run thick with fish. It's a staple of our diet, but this type I have never experienced before.

Boukie takes a huge bite out of the food on her plate and speaks around the mass in her mouth, a thin, white, pasty substance smeared across her lips.

"It's a tuna fish sammich!" she declares with a happy noise, her words running together in her sweet childish lisp. "Nana Lucy makes the bestest sammiches."

"Tuna is a large ocean-dwelling fish," Lucy says. "And the word is sandwich, Boukie."

Boukie frowns up at her. "That's what I said."

She is all smiles again within seconds as she leans forward to whisper, "My mommy makes the *bestest* tuna. It's not a sammich. It's a cassie-ol. It's got noodles, tato chips, and peas." She grimaces. "I don't like peas, but they're okay in tuna cassie-ol. You'll like it. I'll tell Mommy to make it for you."

"That's a great idea, Boukie," I say as I take a bite of my own sandwich. Taste bursts over my tongue. The thin, white food paste has a slightly sweet flavoring that congeals the fish, and a tartness added from some green pickled bits. It all offsets the mild, flaky fish in an appealing way, no less so than the two thin pieces of bread holding it together. This sandwich innovation I must share with my brethren. It is a truly clever and tasty way to concoct a small midday repast.

"Cavek, are you really gonna go back with Orgath and Auntie Sammi?" Boukie asks. I stare at her in surprise and my heart swells. I can't stay, but I don't want to leave without Boukie and Kate. It surely wouldn't go unnoticed by Sammi if I attempted to take them with me.

"Yes, I am," I say.

"Oh," she huffs with disappointment. "Is your home very nice?"

I nod at her a few times. "It *is* very nice. You would like it. It's in the middle of a great forest, with rivers and streams running through it, and there are all kind of wild animals. We build our homes in the roots of the giant trees where we won't disturb them, or sometimes in houses high in the branches. At night, the whole village is lit up with lanterns and faery lights. All the trolls like to dance and sing at night, because we are the best-loved children of the moon."

Boukie's eyes widen. "Wow..." she breathes. "Can I be a troll and live in the troll village?"

I ruffle her dark hair affectionately.

"You would make a fine troll," I say.

"She certainly has the attitude for it," Sammi says as she comes in and sits across from me. She smiles at her niece before fixing a stern look on me. "What are you doing, Cavek?"

My eyes grow wide. "I'm merely enjoying Boukie's company. We have been painting and making our letters."

"Uh-huh. And this has nothing to do with Kate?"

I frown at her. That is not fair.

"I do not like what you are asking. Boukie is a part of Kate—there is no dispute on that—but I enjoy Boukie for herself. She reminds me much of the trollbies, the children in my village. Believe it or not, I enjoy children."

Sammi lowers her eyes and blushes. "I don't mean anything in particular by it. I just want to warn you that you can't get to Kate through her daughter. Men have tried that before, and it didn't go well."

Anger rolls through me just imagining these other men. I do not want to think of my mate and the males she has lain with in the past. In any case, a male who would use a child to gain the favor of a female was loathsome. I could only feel sympathy for Kate for what she's had to deal with coming from the males of her own species. Though I appreciate that Sammi is looking out for her friend, I find that I am equally irritated at her for the assumption that I would do something that vile.

"I assure you that anything between me and Kate will happen because we mutually want it, and no other reason," I say stiffly.

"I'm sorry, Cavek. It's nothing personal, not against you. I just want the best for my friend."

Oh, I understand very well. I understand that I have to be careful and reveal nothing in front of Sammi. Trolls are hunters—predators, really—by nature. I can be patient as I lay the groundwork for my claim.

Folding my hands on the table, I put on a polite smile for Sammi.

CHAPTER 3

CAVEK

When Kate arrives, Sammi's father David strikes up a large metal brazier of sorts that he calls a grill. I'm so fascinated with this barbeque idea that it keeps me moderately entertained so that I am not hovering suspiciously over my female as she socializes with her adoptive family. I do not know what to make of this grill. No doubt it is a curious thing but seems inferior to methods we trolls make use of.

Among trolls, we have a grill, but it is only a metal lacing that we set over a low fire. Containing it in a brazier seems odd to me. Why not just dig a pit, line it with rocks and peat, and place the metal lacing over it? I'm certain if he did it that way, he would find the results far more satisfying. To my surprise, he looks at me with horror when I suggest it, but he offers to let me build a fire in his burn pit for something called marsh-a-mallows after our evening meal.

David is woefully lacking in peat, and I cannot imagine what uncivilized realm I have come to that doesn't give every family a ration of it. My mother sees to the distribution of peat among the trolls herself. I pull the metal lacing out of an old, unused brazier with a rusted bottom and haul it over to the shamefully shallow indention that he calls a burn pit. Boukie trails behind me with a handful of bright ribbons, watching my every move with focused interest.

With great care, I scoop her up and set her on a nearby log.

"Sit here and observe," I instruct her. "I will show you how trolls prepare to do this barbequing thing. First, we must double the depth of the pit. You want it big enough to layer rocks in the bottom and to contain a second layer, either of tall rocks or metal poles, that holds lacing above the fire. This is far too shallow."

Boukie nods. "Yes, too shallow," she parrots sagely.

I grin at my little trollbie. I will make a fine troll out of her.

I make quick work of digging out the pit with my claws. Unlike humans with their flimsy nails, trolls are graced by the gods with thick claws that allow us to dig through most substances with ease. A determined troll with enough time on his hands can even burrow into stone without doing more than slightly dulling his claws.

Once I'm satisfied with the depth, I step out of the pit, brush off the dirt, and begin to scour the wooded area framing the yard for appropriate rocks for my mission. Boukie bounds through the brush and yells whenever she comes across a decently-sized stone. To my relief, I find six large rocks appropriate to position the lacing high enough above the fire.

We get a few odd looks as we haul our rocks out and throw them beside the pit, but for the most part, everyone seems to be interested in what I am doing. Luke and Kate both wander closer as I line the pit with our findings. Boukie hovers like a taskmaster, pointing at what stone I should place next. She's so earnest I refrain from laughing and dutifully do as instructed.

That doesn't stop Kate from chuckling, the sweet sound

warming my heart and spurring my imagination. It doesn't take much effort to think of Kate and I comfortably secure in my tree-burrow, sitting outside its thick roots enjoying this barbequing thing with our children.

It's a nice fantasy.

To my surprise, just as I am about to scout for something I can use in place of peat, David hands me a bag of scented wood chips.

"What is this?"

"I've never had the occasion to use them before. They're hickory-mesquite wood chips."

"Hmm," I mutter speculatively. I have never used wood chips, outside of tossing in random bits of wood into the fire, but in theory it could work well. Besides, I hate to turn away a thoughtful gesture from the human. Especially not when Kate is watching on with such interest. I need to show that I am willing to explore a middle ground between our species. Very well, then.

"Thank you," I say and proceed to line the pit with half the bag before setting the logs carefully on top of the chips. To my delight, I find a bit of dry moss that I place at one side for kindling. As I remove the steel and flint from my pouch, I crouch down low beside the pit and strike them, sending sparks down onto the moss.

I chuckle when Kate makes an excited noise as a spark catches onto the kindling. She grins and blushes with embarrassment, but her small noise is overshadowed by Boukie's squeals as she jumps up and down, clapping her hands in excitement.

"Cavek made a fire, Mommy!" Boukie crows as she dances around at a safe distance from the fire pit. "He did it like magic!"

I lean forward with a grin and ask her, "Do you want to see some real magic?"

Boukie's eyes widen further as she nods.

Chuckling, I double-check to make certain that there are no low hanging tree branches that would accidentally catch on fire.

Then, I lean forward and whisper into the flames as I weave the subtle energies around me into a simple illusion enchantment. I lean back just in time to avoid the tiny burst of flames sending up sparks of butterflies several inches into the air before fading out harmlessly.

I laugh as Boukie shouts in delight at the fiery butterflies, but my laughter dies in my throat when I meet Kate's eyes. There's a certain appreciation in her gaze as she watches me that makes my blood instantly run hot. I yearn to move toward her, pull her braid free, and run my fingers through her dark hair.

Someone has initiated the music from the radio box that Jake showed me yesterday. It's marvelous, and the music adds depth to the wanderings of my imagination. I can see myself stripping her clothes from her body in time to the heavy beat of the music—

A tiny hand wraps around three of my fingers and my attention is pulled down to the smiling face of the tiny female. She lifts her arms over her head and smiles ever so sweetly at me.

"Dance with me," she says winsomely as she rocks from side to side, her ponytails swaying with the motion.

Although I'd been jolted out of my fantasy, I cannot find it within me to be annoyed. Rather, I feel a warmth inside my chest and an irresistible smile tugging at my lips. I lift one of her hands and bow over it.

"I cannot resist such a request made by a lovely trollbie as yourself," I declare in my most exaggerated courtly manner.

Boukie giggles as I pull her up off the ground in my arms and swing her around in a popular stomping dance.

"What's a trollbie?" she says between peals of sweet laughter.

I swing her around in an arc before I reply. "It is the word that means a troll child."

"I'm not a troll, silly!"

I pause in my step and feign surprise.

"No? Are you certain? You seem quite like a troll to me."

"I wanna be a troll!" she shrieks as I set her down at the end of the song. I tell her again that she will be a fine troll as she turns to let everyone know just that fact.

Lucy pauses as she sets plates on the wooden table and looks down at her.

"Boukie, really? A troll? Wouldn't you rather be... I don't know... a princess?"

The little one pauses to think for a second and then nods her head emphatically.

"Yes, Nana. A *troll* princess," she says, and it pleases me to no end.

I turn to find Kate once more, but to my disappointment she's gone. As the fire builds, I turn my attention back to it, waiting for the flames to die down enough to safely cook over. Kate still hasn't emerged from the house a short time later when I start to add slabs of steaks onto the metal lacing. I struggle to restrain myself from grumbling.

On the porch, David sets narrow, unappealing meat tubes on his grill. I can't help but notice that the orcs are gravitating to my fire pit, although the younger orc, who appears to be enjoying the company of Sammi's younger brother, gamely eats the hot dog offered to him. The humans thankfully miss the collective looks of disgust as the rest of us watch on in horror, which only increase when the orc declares it "not bad" and reaches for another.

When Kate emerges, she's with Sammi, carrying bowls of food from the house to the large wooden tables. Unlike the table indoors, these are spacious enough to seat all of our company. They speak as close companions, laughing and teasing as they set the food out. As Kate sets her last bowl down, she turns to look at me from beneath her lashes. That glance is so heated that my skin tingles as if electrified or attacked by some enchantment.

The orc beside me bellows that the meat is burning, throwing me out of my stupor to rescue the juicy cuts. One side has a darker sear than anticipated, but they survived well enough. I pile the steaks on the platter beside me and bring it to the tables. I'm the last to arrive but nonetheless highly appreciated for the offering I bring with me.

∼

Kate

I wiggle in seat as Cavek sits beside me. He smells like woodsmoke, rugged and spicy. I nearly choked on my lust when I came out with Sammi and saw him at the fire. At some point, he'd taken off his shirt while he'd been cooking over the fire, and all I could see were miles of defined green muscle.

My interest must have been pretty obvious, because Sammi had felt it her responsibility to remind me once again to be careful playing with a non-human man. Sitting so close to him now, I'm struggling to keep in mind how potentially dangerous and unsuitable a fling with him could be.

It's all I can do to function like a normal person and eat the food in front of me while trying to ignore the fluttering interest in my belly. I know Cavek is aware of it. As soon as he sat beside me, his nostrils flared, and he made a toe-curling growl deep in his throat. All that did was make me impossibly, embarrassingly wet. I'm pretty sure the orcs are aware too, if the sly looks the pair of brothers is giving me are anything to go by.

At least my fellow humans are blissfully unaware. I don't think I could face the teasing Sammi's brothers, Jake and Luke, would lay on me. And I have no doubt that they would. Ever since Lucy practically adopted me, they haven't failed to treat me like another sister. Sometimes, it's fun, but other times it's extremely embarrassing.

I'm so distracted I barely taste the food I eat. It might as well have been cardboard. I'm certain this is just an inconvenient itch that needs to be scratched. Yes, it's a really bad idea to scratch that particular itch with a troll, but no one else is going to satisfy it. Besides, they're leaving soon. When will I ever have another opportunity? Cavek seems more than a little interested in a bit of fun between the sheets.

I don't know how to approach him about it, though. I may be bold with men, but all my nerve has dried up facing the mass of sex appeal and magic that is Cavek. He isn't just another sexy man; this guy, even with his fondness for things sharp and deadly, is fascinating, funny, and genuinely enjoys Boukie without using her to come on to me. It makes my ovaries sit up and take notice, much to my dismay. I'm not looking for a daddy for Boukie—or a daddy for more babies—but I can't deny that Cavek would make a great dad.

After dinner, I let my little imp run around until she exhausts herself and then I hustle out of there with Boukie in tow before I say or do something very, very stupid. Like 'trip over my tongue and the trail of drool Cavek inspires' stupid. Boukie protests but is tired enough from the excitement of the day that her argument doesn't last long before she's out cold in the car. She barely stirs when I lift her out of her seat, and even less so when I strip her down and pull her into a nightgown before putting her to bed.

One thing I can say for Boukie: she may be hell on wheels when she's awake, but she sleeps like a log.

After a satisfying stretch, I turn to the kitchen and pull out the rum from the freezer to make myself a lazy girl's daiquiri. This is my go-to when I want something alcoholic but am too tired to bother with the blender. I just pour the daiquiri mix straight into a glass with the chilled alcohol and—bam—it's ready.

Setting my cup on the side table, I lie on the couch, allowing myself to relax as my imagination frolics all over Cavek's wonderfully delicious bod. Before long, my fingers slip into my panties. I lean back, imagining just what Cavek hides beneath his pants and the noises he might make as he drives into me, as I stroke myself to completion. The orgasm comes fast and strong, but it's not as satisfying as I would have hoped.

With a disgruntled groan, I flick on the TV and bolt upright when a televised Humans First meeting pops on. These lunatics have been holding meetings and low-key protests since the fae made contact, but they've never even so much as whispered a suggestion of violence. Suddenly, the orcs are hot news and I watch with morbid fascination and mounting horror as more than one person in the audience shouts for violent insurrection against the "ungodly monsters" coming into the human realm.

There's no way they would be stupid enough to attack orcs and a troll. But as the program ends, I can't help but feel unease in the pit of my stomach. Something in my gut tells me I should call Sammi, and I reach for my cell phone. Maybe talking to her will set my mind to ease about it. She'll probably just laugh at my concerns and tell me that they're just blowing hot air. She never takes protest groups seriously.

Fuck. Looking at my phone's clock, it's already after midnight. Tomorrow, then. I'll talk to her about it tomorrow. I'm probably just being paranoid. That must be it.

CHAPTER 4

KATE

To my frustration, Sammi wasn't home when I finally pulled myself out of bed. I'd woken up with Boukie's hair in my mouth. At some point during the early morning, she'd crawled into bed with me without waking me. It's something we've been working on, but every now and then she winds up in bed with me again.

As soon as I untangled myself, I called the house and was informed quite pleasantly by Luke that Sammi went out baby shopping with Lucy and the only female orc of the group, Erra. It still blows my mind to think of Sammi pushing out a half-orc baby here in a few months. And I thought all six pounds of Boukie had been rough!

"Well, is Cavek there?" I ask. Maybe he could help allay my fears.

"Uh, no," Luke says apologetically. "Sorry, Kate. I'm the only one home right now. Cavek went with the girls to be their pack mule," he chortled a bit with evil glee at that and even I winced with sympathy, "and Jake took the guys out to IHOP. He said it was an American experience they couldn't miss. Something about all-you-can-eat pancakes."

"Have you seen anything from the human rights activists?" I hedged, hoping maybe if nothing else Luke would have some opinion on the matter to set me at ease.

"Nah. Sorry, Kate. You know I don't watch that crap. I hate to waste brain space on their paranoia. I know Jake likes to follow that stuff, though, and he keeps the rest of us informed whether we like it or not."

Huh. Maybe Jake will be of better help. I grab a scrap of paper and a pen.

"Do you have Jake's cell number? I'll shoot him a text."

Luke rattles off a string of numbers that I scribble down, and we disconnect after I assure him that I will be over for dinner to help out again tonight with feeding everyone. I tap my pen on the counter beside me as I punch in Jake's number and a quick message.

Jake, any news on Humans First? Did you see last night's meeting on TV?

It takes Jake only a moment to get back to me. Gods bless that blogger for always having his phone at hand.

Nah, went to bed early and missed it. Will check it out when I get home. U OK?

Yeah, all good here. Just worried.

Will look ASAP, promise.

Thanks, Jake.

I set my phone down and stare off into space, unsure of what to do. I could call Lucy, see where they are, and join them. But Sammi has Cavek and Erra with her. I doubt anyone will actually try anything with those two around.

Knowing that there's really nothing I can do right now, I toss a coffee pod into my Keurig and resolve to enjoy my day off. There are plenty of things I can do around the house until I have the opportunity to talk with everyone later. Unfortunately, even the warm smell of toffee-infused coffee doesn't do anything to lift my spirits.

I scroll through my Facebook feed, trying to kill time and do a little research. No one seems to be talking about the Humans First meeting there either, much to my disappointment.

I'm about to close the app but pause when an ad pops up announcing that the local PetSmart is having an adoption drive today at noon. I rub my shoulder as I stare at the picture of a litter of fuzzy kittens. Sammi said she wanted to take a kitten back to the orc village. Maybe that would be the perfect present for her. Who knows if she would even have time to go herself? Especially if people start acting crazy.

That settles it.

"Boukie, come eat breakfast. We're going out today," I say as her little tangled mop of hair comes into view.

Cavek

Four hours of shopping with three females. I have no idea how I was talked into this. I should have known better. I have been shopping before with my mother and my two sisters. Shopping with females is never good news for any male accompanying them.

As we shop, I also make some note of it myself just in case I am blessed with trollbies of my own. I never knew babies needed so much. But then again, I am not only the third son but also the youngest of my mother's brood. I have never so much as seen a babe up close, since none of my siblings have yet to reproduce despite all being mated.

Still, it's not a total loss. Especially not when Lucy announces it is time for the midday meal, and we stop at a place called Thai Palace in their multi-level bazaar. As soon as we step inside, I'm assaulted by the most wondrous smells.

The elderly lady who greets us gives me a long look, but it seems more like she's sizing up how much food she can feed me rather than particularly fearful. I recognize this familiar look. It is the gimlet eye of every serious food industry proprietor across both dimensions, it seems. I have plenty of gold coin with me; I have no problem parting with any of it for a full belly of good tasting food. Like all trolls, I love to eat.

I am a bit dismayed when I am handed a menu. I look at it hopelessly until Sammi grins and plucks it out of my hands.

"Allow me to order something for you," Sammi offers, and I am both grateful and suspicious. Fortunately, not only do trolls love to eat but we also possess stomachs likened to cast-iron pits. It's hard to even so much as poison us, and we willingly eat most anything. Although, the hot dogs were a personal exception for me. I can't imagine that stuff even qualifies as food. Still, I doubt there is anything Sammi can order for me that I won't enjoy, so I just nod and smile with gratitude.

To my surprise and delight given my more massive size, she orders three plates of food for me and almost as much for Erra. Any suspicion I felt at having her order is vaporized when my plates are set in front of me. I inhale and am hit with the intoxicating aroma of heat and spice. I smack my lips, and I can almost taste the burst of spice and flavors over my tongue.

The first mouthful hits just right. The heat strikes first, yet the complexity of the flavor is so different from anything I have experienced it ensnares me. I recognize the meat well enough—bits of chicken and beef—but the peppers and spices are completely different than what grows in the cooler forest climates of Ov'Gorg that I call home.

The colors are unique too. Bright vegetables in red or green sauces. The red curry is less spicy but by far my favorite. The whole experience is so enjoyable that I clean every bit of food off my own plate and happily eat the scraps of remaining pad thai on Sammi and Lucy's plates.

I am still pleasantly licking the flavor off my fangs and relishing the lingering heat in my mouth when we return to shopping. Admittedly, a good meal puts me in a far more pleasant mood, so I don't immediately feel an impulse to kill the first human who starts shouting absurdities down at us from the level above. It's almost entertaining that they think all they have to do is make a bit of noise at us and that we would go fleeing in terror.

It isn't until the humans start directing profanities at Sammi and calling her a whore that I bristle and glare up at the cowardly males jeering out of reach. I start to look for a way up there when suddenly we are pelted with food. Although some of it smells quite nice, the insult is clear.

I snarl and prepare to retaliate when Lucy takes the situation in hand and herds us all out of there. It's with great reluctance that I follow the matronly female out of the multi-level bazaar. I would rather stay and fight, and Erra also looks like she would rather go back inside and start splitting heads open.

I recognize that this is probably for the best. I don't want Orgath's little human mate getting caught in any potential crossfire. Knowing her temperament, Sammi would want to be in the thick of any fighting. Retreating is the more responsible decision.

Kate

When I finally pull up later in the day, I'm armed with a little orange ball of fluff. For a minute there, I hadn't been sure if we were ever going to get out of the pet store. We'd chosen a kitten and were preparing to leave with our charge when we encountered the puppy pen. Within five minutes, Boukie had every puppy in the pen crawling onto her lap. She'd taken one look at the puppies around her and lost her heart. It took twenty minutes of begging to get her out of there without taking home any other furry friends.

My landlord barely tolerates the fact I have an active child in my apartment. He's definitely not going to let me bring home the eight-week-old Great Dane pup that Boukie clung to with big tear-filled eyes. It took a solemn oath, extracted with a pinky swear, that we would get a puppy when we had a bigger place to live for Boukie to finally part from the wiggling mass of dogs.

All it took was two messages from Jake as I was leaving PetSmart with Boukie to make me go from nervous to full-on scared. One to say that he'd been researching the matter and things were worse than I'd thought, and the second to verify that I'm coming over tonight.

Is this it? My best friend is going to have to leave. Who knows if I'll ever see her again? And then there's Cavek. There's a certain finality about things when I think of him that leaves a sinking feeling in my stomach. I miss Sammi already, but I'm having a hard time even imagining that I'll never have the chance to see Cavek again. Even if by some miracle I manage to stay in touch with Sammi, she lives in the orc village, not among the trolls.

What I have tonight will likely be all I will ever have with him.

I'm not stupid. I know that our relationship has no future. It's lust born of natural curiosity and not much else. Truthfully, we haven't even had the opportunity to begin a relationship, really. Now everything is coming to a swift end. It makes no sense that I even care. Even Boukie seems to be subdued with some innate understanding that things weren't quite right.

To my mortification, I can barely keep my tears in check when I gracelessly shove the tiny kitten into my best friend's hands. She looks at it for a long moment and then Sammi also has to try not to cry. Luke's assurances that he'll help us exchange letters every month is the only thing that finally allows us to pull ourselves together. This cross-dimensional shit isn't really going to separate us much. It'll just be like the old days when people had to wait weeks for mail carriers.

The good old days, when people traveled by covered wagons... Fuck.

Despite the serious nature of the occasion, everyone is doing their best to keep their spirits high. The boys are roughhousing in the yard, and everyone is loud and boisterous. Despite all the noise, Boukie is already passed out in Orgath's arms, and I find myself searching for and meeting the eyes of Cavek.

Everything in me screams to be bold and daring... and then completely fails. Since when am I timid around men? Apparently, since now. I wipe my sweaty hands on the sides of my jeans and step back into the safety of the house.

I crack open one of Lucy's fruity wine coolers and lean against the kitchen counter, watching as Sammi sits beside her hulking mate and leans forward to whisper something into his ear that makes the male grin.

I smile at the sight. Sammi deserves a good guy.

"They look happy," a familiar deep voice says behind me.

I resist the urge to turn around and look at Cavek. The male doesn't give up, though, and he reaches forward to set his hand upon mine. I look down at the long green finger tipped with curved black claws and feel a flutter in my belly at the contrast of his larger hand over my much smaller one. His other hand settles on the counter, on the other side of me, and I can feel his breath hot on my neck as if he's drawing in my scent. My mouth goes dry but somehow, I manage to turn and face him in the cage of his arms.

I pointedly glance down at his arms and raise my eyebrows at him. Cavek leans back slightly, a wicked smile curving his dark lips and showing a hint of his fangs, but he doesn't release me.

I take a long sip from my drink, allowing the tart flavors to flow over my tongue as study the features and colors of his intriguing face. He pulls off purple and green better than Jack Nicholson in *Batman*, and that was an intriguing combination.

"They do," I say in agreement. "I don't know Orgath very well, but I know Sammi deserves every bit of the happiness she's found with him."

Cavek tilts his head and eyes me with curiosity.

"Even though he's not human?"

I shrug. "Perhaps human is overrated."

His laughter is almost like a purr, and his amethyst eyes sparkle at me in the dim lighting.

"And what do *you* deserve, Kate?" he drawls.

"At this point in my life, I can't be worried about what I want or deserve. I had that chance, but now I have Boukie. What I need is to find what's best for her."

He turns his head to look at Boukie, his long lavender hair brushing my cheek as he does so. I inhale the complex scent of him as the hairs tickle my nose. Cavek nods his head as he considers my words.

"I can understand that. Trolls value children above all other things. We are notorious for making off with abandoned babes we find at the borders of our woods and raising them among our own young. The needs of children must always be a priority."

He glances down at me, his expression earnest. "But that doesn't mean that they replace our needs as individual beings. That we neglect our own happiness."

I have no idea what to say to counter that, so instead I ask, "What do you deserve then, Cavek? What will make you happy?"

"Something and someone to call my own," he replies so seriously I know he's not just shamelessly flirting or being his usual cavalier self. "I am the youngest of many children and most everything and everyone in my life I have had to share with siblings. I want my own home. My own family. A mate," he clarifies slowly.

A grin spreads on his face, breaking the solemnity of the moment. "And if that gets my mother off my back, all the better."

I laugh in relief.

"Ah, yes, matchmaking mothers. I take it this is a problem among trolls too then?"

Cavek shudders.

"Troll mothers are the worst of all species on Ov'Gorg. They want all their children to be mated and producing trollbies to fill their arms. The bigger the family, the happier the troll."

"So all the mating and making babies are to please your mothers?" I giggle, finishing the wine cooler with a gulp.

His smile widens. "I wouldn't quite say that. What I feel for you right at this moment certainly has nothing to do with my mother."

"Oh... Well, I'm relieved to hear it," I say in a breathy voice, excitement stirring in my breast. I lick my lips. I have no idea how long Boukie is going to stay asleep, but this feels like a now or never moment.

Everything within me is on board. He's sweet, funny... and I can't forget deadly. He's the epitome of the bad boy who every nineties teen lusted over—the one who a good number of grown women still lust over, if they're being honest with themselves.

My eyelashes drift down as I peer at him, my pussy clamoring for attention.

"Seeing how we're both on the same page... it wouldn't hurt to indulge ourselves," I say.

"A most excellent idea," he leans in and whispers. My skin tingles with excitement from the brush of his breath on my ear seconds before his tongue sweeps out to trace the rounded edge, so different from the long and narrow taper of his own ears.

I feel his arms wrap around me and he lifts me off my feet as his hot lips plaster to my neck. Without ceremony, he carries me into the guest room and gently deposits me on several thick blankets stretched out over the floor.

I have the feeling that this is where he sleeps. The blankets smell of him, wondrously so. I wonder if Lucy would notice if I snuck one of them out after he leaves. My heart lurches at the thought of him leaving.

Before I can dwell on it, my mind drifts along with the onslaught of passion he raises within me with every kiss and nip he delivers upon my skin.

My hands seem to belong to a wild, unreasonable creature as I pull the lacings of his shirt free and, with his eager assistance, yank it off Cavek's muscular torso. My fingers trail down his perfectly defined abs, exploring with wonder until I arrive at the laces holding his pants shut. I unlace these as well and am barely patient enough for him to shuck them before I take the length of him in my greedy hands.

The breath empties out of my lungs as I gaze upon his sex. It's two shades darker in hue and studded all up the length with tiny, knobby bumps. The head is thick and only slightly tapered, making it appear even bigger. But that's not what makes my mouth drop open. The tip of it is pierced in a reversed prince albert. I've never seen one in the flesh before, much less been with a man who had his dick pierced. My mouth goes dry and my pussy dampens further, imagining the feel of it sliding within me.

Cavek's deep chuckle is my only warning before I'm swept against him once more, his head lowering so he can consume my mouth with his as we rub belly-to-belly, pelvis-to-pelvis.

I know instinctively that his passion is running as high as mine. There will be no foreplay, no clever touches designed to drive each other out of our minds. There's only the mindless frenzy of need. I relish, welcome, and anticipate the wild rush of our coming together.

His cock rubs against my folds twice before he delves deep into me, my pussy clenching against the thick intrusion of him. He gives me space to adjust, but the moment I squirm with rebuilding passion he thrusts into me, grinding deeply at each pass. My breath comes in pants as he builds our tempo, our hips colliding against each other in nature's unbridled affirmation of life.

Each thrust is so deep I feel it all through me as if he's determined to become a part of me. Gods help me, I want that too. I want to keep him inside me and never let him go.

He pulls my legs up to give him better leverage and thrusts deeper and faster into me. I can barely keep up with him as I rock my hips in time with his rhythm. Sweat pours off us, mingling in the places we touch. Cavek growls over me, the volume increasing as his pace does, until I hear a loud rumble echoing in the room as he lifts me flush against him and pounds at an inhuman speed into me.

I throw my head back, prepared to scream as my orgasm rips through me, but my cries are swallowed as Cavek descends upon my mouth again, thrusting his long tongue into my mouth. To my surprise, this takes my orgasm even further and I tremble with its intensity before we crash back down to Earth again, our bodies sliding off each other as we fall onto the blankets.

"Wow…" I breathe.

"Indeed," he murmurs as he turns ever so slightly to kiss the top of my head.

CHAPTER 5

CAVEK

She's not coming. The realization dawns as we mount and prepare to leave in the early hours with the light barely cresting over the mountains. As everyone loads onto their mounts, I glance down the road every so often, hoping to catch sight of Kate's small red transport. I do not even realize that I am being obvious until I meet the sympathetic gaze of Bodi from where he sits on his massive delfass.

I stare morosely down at the thick fur of my mount as my heart sinks into the pit of my stomach. I know she is my blood-bond, but I have to wonder if she feels so little of it that it's easy for her to dismiss me from her life. We shared amazing passion, and my entire being yearns for her. Maybe she doesn't feel anything.

The whole thing leaves a sour taste in my mouth.

I'm a troll; I'm a warrior and a prince. I am powerful. I am not used to feeling uncertain and vulnerable. I don't like it. I resolve to harden my heart and take what is mine, but then my heart leaps pathetically in my chest like that of an eager youth when I see her vehicle pull up.

My entire world narrows down to my female as she runs to me, Boukie in her arms. I can hear the scoffing sounds coming from Erra. She'd been the only one I had confided my anxiety to as we were preparing to leave. She'd assured me then that Kate would come, though I didn't hide my doubt over her conviction.

She has every reason to scoff at me now that she is proven right, and I will not hold it against her that she enjoys her victory.

I slide off my borrowed delfass and enclose my arms around them, breathing in the sweet smells of my females, my mate, and my daughter. Kate's soft body clings to me and tears dampen my cheek where it is pressed against hers. Boukie's arms slide around my neck, anchoring me to her. Determination solidifies within me.

This is my family. I have to leave for now with Orgath as promised, but I will return for them.

Kate pulls back, her eyes red and swimming with tears as she sets a hand on my arm. "I'm going to miss you," she whispers, her lips curving into a bittersweet smile. "Promise me I'll see you again someday."

I can't help but smile. My sweet Kate doesn't realize just how soon and forever that will be. I nod my head once and gently unwind Boukie from around me, her cries dying down into pitiful whimpers as she stares at me from her mother's arms.

Kate takes her from me before reaching up one hand to grab a thick lock of hair, pulling my head down to her as she stands on her toes so that her lips may capture mine. The kiss is sweet, a promise of things to come the next time we meet.

With a final shaky smile, Kate squeezes Boukie to her and walks back to her car. As she leans against the car, Kate still watches me, as I watch her. I mount the delfass once again, never breaking my focus from her. In the final moments of this gray morning neither of us wish to take our eyes off the other. This moment will have to last until I am able to return, so I do not wish to waste even a second of it.

Not even when Orgath gives the command do I take my eyes from my mate. I squeeze my legs around my mount's thick torso and he obediently follows behind the other delfass mounted by the orcs. In time, she becomes a blurry outline, and there is a strange moisture in my eyes that I scrub out impatiently. Then finally all I can see is the bright red outline of her car before that too is swallowed into the distance.

∼

Kate

My heart beats painfully as I watch the giant felines disappear from sight carrying away my best friend and the one guy who was able to completely turn my world upside down. I bite my lip.

I never should have slept with him. Now that I have, I can't bear the thought of any other man touching me. Not only do I doubt anyone could ever measure up, everything within me is repulsed by the idea. Cavek will go on with his life and find a troll princess or something to settle down with. This inspires foreign feelings of hostility. Instead of my usual post-fling apathy, the very idea of Cavek finding a nice troll lady to settle down with makes me grind my teeth together.

I'm not the type to get jealous over other women, especially not over such a brief encounter. I've never seen the sense in women fighting over men, nor have I cried over a cheating scumbag. It's always been so easy to cut men out of my life, so why is it this hard to say goodbye to Cavek?

"Don't worry, Mommy. Cavek is gonna come back for us," Boukie says softly.

I look over at her and furrow my brow.

"What do you mean, baby?"

"He says he's coming back," she says into my shoulder, half-asleep. "He says Imma gonna be a troll princess for reals." She finishes on a yawn just before she falls back to sleep.

I sigh and remain silent. Later, we can have the talk about how grown-ups sometimes say things that aren't true to make parting easier and to bring a little bit of happiness. But that won't be today.

Today, she watched Cavek leave us.

Today, she can enjoy her dream that someday he'll return for us and she'll get to be a troll princess.

CHAPTER 6

CAVEK

*D*ays have gone by since I have seen my bloodbond and instead of initiating my plan to abscond with her, I am once again trying not to sigh as my father frowns at me from his throne. His heavy brow is furrowed with obvious displeasure, all because I said I didn't have time to go with my older brother Serus and fight the northern werewolf tribe bordering our territory.

I really don't see what the problem is. Serus is more than capable, as he likes to remind me, and I have more important things that require my attention. Like my mate, for instance. It's not like I didn't turn him down politely.

My mother sighs on her gnarled wooden throne at his side, giving voice to my feelings at this moment but for an entirely different reason. She doesn't like it when my father's plans for me conflict with hers. Her schemes have never been pleasant, so I'm not particularly eager for either option.

I just want to get this over with so I can return to my female.

Mother taps her fingers impatiently on the arm of her throne. The dress she wears is the most hideous pink masterpiece I believe I've ever seen created by the local pixie hive. I don't blame the pixies. Their textiles are the best in all of the Middling Way Kingdom. No, it's my mother's sense of taste and doubtless colorblindness at fault.

An emerald green troll in such a brilliant shade of pink is... unsettling.

Unfortunately, it's her favorite color and she insists everything for her be made in some variation of the hue. Her lavender hair hangs loose over her shoulders and down her back. Only a troll going into battle will bind their hair, and Mother prides herself on having the wildest locks.

Father rubs his brow as he scowls. I am always the disappointment for our father. I learned to fight—and learned it well—to make him proud. Truthfully, I enjoy a good brawl for the fun of it like most trolls. However, when it comes to actual problems, I am not so quick to think that brute force is the only way to deal with it.

I have been trying for months to get Father to agree to seek peace talks with the werewolf tribes who border our kingdom to no avail. He only sees my suggestions as a sign of weakness. Trolls don't back down from fights. If another being wants a fight, trolls gladly oblige and make them regret it.

"Cavek, enough!" he growls. "Enough of this gallivanting around already. You have duties at home that you have yet to tend to. I know you enjoy playing envoy when the opportunity arises, but it is time to take your responsibilities seriously. Appease your mother, take a mate, and defend our territories. It is not a difficult thing we ask, Cavek."

Serus snickers behind me.

I shoot my oldest brother a murderous look but turn beseeching eyes on my mother.

"Mother, please. I cannot go with Serus. I need to return to Ov'Ge. I have found my mate."

"Cavek," Father begins but Mother leaps from her throne, interrupting him.

"Virol, hush. Didn't you hear him? He has found a mate. We cannot possibly send him to fight werewolves."

"Madi, my love. You were not listening when he said that his mate is in Ov'Ge. She is human. I am sure she will make a fine addition to our family, but our first responsibility is to protect our people and our young. She will be perfectly safe waiting in Ov'Ge."

I try to keep my expression neutral rather than glare at my father as he returns his attention to me.

"Cavek, aid Serus in pushing back the northern Warue Tribe and you have my permission to return to Ov'Ge to fetch your mate."

I grind my teeth but know that this is the best offer I'm going to get. Mother pouts but does not argue with Father's decision. With a short nod that toes the line of being respectful, I turn and stalk out of the throne room. I do not acknowledge my brother following after me until Serus comes up beside me and slaps me on the back.

"Cheer up, Cavek. We will go kick some wolf tail and will be back in time for the morning meal. You will be mated and have your own female nagging at your dirty boots on her clean floors before you know it."

I roll my eyes. Serus's mate is a sweet female. I know good and well that he tracks mud over her floors just to get a rise out of her and to give some heat to their love life. Not that it was a detail I particularly needed him to share with me. I do *not* wish to envision my brother naked with his mate.

Without a word, I return to my room and lash myself into my leather armor. I forego the heavy metal breastplate my brothers prefer, since the extra bulk makes it difficult for me to draw my bow at a moment's notice. The chest and belly area are covered with gold-trimmed green scales gifted to me by a dragon I aided in my youth, making it, in my opinion, far superior. I know my brother is impatient to be underway, so I strap on my knives and quiver before snatching up my bow and hurrying out the door.

∼

My brother underestimated the determination of the Warue Tribe. That's the first thing that occurs to me when I wake many hours later, my body pained from the rigorous battle, in a dark cell. The second thing I'm aware of is that I've been stripped bare, without even a scrap of cloth to give me any comfort or preserve my pride. I hear the scamper of a rodent and blink my eyes as I try to adjust to the low lighting. It takes a few minutes, but eventually I can make out my surroundings.

The walls seem earthen, although reinforced by stone and metal. The cell itself is lined with iron, effective for holding a troll since it mitigates our magic. The only way out seems to be through brute strength alone, and I doubt even that will be successful.

I narrow my eyes and follow the lines of the bars keeping me caged in, looking for any possible weak spots. If I could find a patch of exposed earth, it would take little effort for me to dig it free from where it's anchored. But the wolves were smart enough to foresee that method of escape.

The door bursts open with a bang, drawing my attention to a large furred body passing through it. The werewolf is black as night with a long, thick tail trailing behind him. I know immediately that this is the alpha, the strongest of the tribe. He'd been leading the attack before I was attacked from behind and knocked unconscious.

Trophies from his conquests, most of them fangs of various shapes and sizes, adorn a thick braid of hair hanging behind one ear and around his neck. The lips of his muzzle part to reveal his own massive, sharp teeth.

"Cavek, son of Virol, such a pleasure to finally make your acquaintance. I hope that the cell is comfortable," he says with a snort.

The pair of males behind him bark out coarse laughter as their alpha picks up a curved knife.

"This is how things will go," he continues, admiring his blade all the while. "You tell us what we want to know, and we will let you go... eventually. You don't? Well, you get a lot of pain and enjoy an extended stay in our accommodations."

I grit my teeth. "What exactly do you want to know?"

"Ah, not so fast. First, a little pain to encourage the truth to flow."

I manage to endure the first cuts stoically, but breath hisses out of me as they multiply. I want desperately to black out and stop the pain as I feel a bit of flesh peeled off me. My eyelids droop and I'm close to losing consciousness, but a bucket of cold water is thrown on me.

The alpha sits back and grins at me.

"Now that I have your attention, you will reveal the location of the hidden entrance to the Middling Way Kingdom."

I grin at him, swallowing my exhaustion and agony with great effort.

"Fuck you."

The alpha's ears flatten for a moment but then he begins to chuckle unpleasantly.

"Fuck *me*? No, not quite," he says with a growl as he gestures to one of his wolves out of my line of vision. I feel a hand grip the back of my neck and hot breath fans my shoulder.

I brace myself for the worst. When the pain comes, it lasts

through the night, and I roar until my throat is hoarse before they finally relent and throw me in a cell. The last thing I hear before I succumb to the blessed darkness is laughter.

"Mercol is done with this one. He says to keep him here until he thinks of a better use for him. Poor bastard. Trolls are stubborn beasts. He should have given up what he knew. Now he'll probably die down here."

I draw my legs up, my body protesting the tearing pain in my haunches and the searing pain of the torn flesh on my torso as I curl into myself. My mind, grasping for comfort and relief, conjures with images of Kate. Sweet Kate. I can almost taste her, and I shiver alone in the damp cell, longing to be with her.

Sometime later, a chunk of meat is thrown unceremoniously onto the floor beside me. I gag at the spoiled odor coming off it. Pushing aside my disgust, I reach for it, but I cannot suppress my nausea as I bring it to my face. I gag again but manage to tear off a bite of meat, trying not to taste it as I swallow it down. My stomach curdles but I will survive.

I will survive this and return to my Kate.

~

Kate

I frown and look at the little plastic stick on the bathroom counter in front of me. One time, just one time in years I don't use a condom and two months later, I'm a basket case as I wait for confirmation of what I suspect. I haven't been feeling well lately and a bit of hasty math had me running out to the drug store.

I let out a breath as two blue lines become visible. I'm pregnant, and this time by an actual troll, not just a guy who gets his kicks dressing up as one. I nervously lick my lips. Termination is out of the question for me. That would probably be the easiest solution, especially this early on. Having a troll's baby will undeniably bring a whole slew of new problems on top of the stress of caring for another child.

Still, my heart rebels against it. I couldn't terminate Boukie, and I can't do it this time either.

All the same, I don't know how I'm going to get through this. I lean over the counter and cradle my head in my hands as I battle a fresh wave of morning sickness mixed with a good old-fashioned dose of anxiety.

I'm barely making ends meet as it is. How am I going to care for a baby who'll likely come with an entire set of unknown special needs? I breathe through the panic.

I can do this. We'll manage and he or she will be loved. That's the most important thing. I'm scared shitless, but we'll be okay.

Thump, thump.

Someone knocks on the bathroom door and my entire body stiffens.

"Kate, dear, are you okay in there?" Lucy asks.

"Yeah, I'm all right. Just one sec. I'm coming out."

"Okay, sweetie. I have dinner on the table. Come eat something before you take Boukie home."

I smile. "Thanks, Mom."

"No need to be thanking me. Just hurry before it gets cold."

"Yes, ma'am."

I throw the pregnancy test into the trash can and wash my hands. I need to tell Cavek. I'm sure if I ask Luke, he'll be glad to give Sammi a letter to pass along to Cavek. But I don't know what good that will do.

Boukie still insists he's going to come back for us despite my gentle discouragement of her fantasy. I don't want to acknowledge the sharp pain that lodges in my chest every time she mentions his imminent return. After two months with no word from him, it seems pretty clear he isn't coming back.

I sigh out loud as I open the door and head toward the dining room. If I'm going to ask Luke to take a letter to Sammi, I'm going to have to tell Lucy. She'll never forgive me if she's the last to find out about the baby.

Pulling out a chair, I sit across from Luke as Lucy passes down a plate with a large helping of shepherd's pie. My heart warms at the good memories triggered by the warm, homey smells of the food. This is one of my favorite childhood meals. I blink back tears as I take a bite.

"Kate, is something wrong?" David inquires gently.

I don't want to burden them. They already do so much for me.

"I'm pregnant," I blurt out.

Lucy slowly blinks.

"Oh, well... a baby." Then she smiles brilliantly. "Well, at least I'll have one of my daughters around to spoil. Who's the father? Anyone we know?"

"Ah, yes, you've met him. The father is Cavek."

Her mouth drops open, but Luke has no problem opening his fat mouth.

"Seriously? First, Sammi gets knocked up by an orc, and now you by a troll. What's with this crazy family?" he gripes.

"Imma gonna have a baby brother!" Boukie exclaims, fixating on what she considers the most important detail.

Lucy purses her lips. "Well... that's unexpected, but we will manage. First things first: I insist that you give notice to your landlord and move into Sammi's old room. Boukie can take the guest room. It makes more sense for you to be here with us where we can help you. Then we'll need to find some private medical care for you. Maybe we can see if Orgath can have someone from their world sent to stay with us until you deliver. If word gets around you're carrying a troll's baby, it might not be a good thing."

I nod slowly. What she says makes sense.

Lucy sets her hand on mine gently.

"Don't you worry."

I resolve to follow her advice and take one day at a time. One day becomes another and before I know it, months have passed and the only thing that's changed is that my stomach is about the size of a beach ball. Lucy swears I'm carrying a boy since she carried both her sons straight out in the front. We don't know for sure, since we don't have access to ultrasounds, but the dwarfish midwife is a gods-send. She's modified my diet to provide the best nutrition for a troll fetus and checks on the baby's growth daily.

The only thing that pains me is that there's no word from Cavek. All of my letters have gone unanswered. Sammi assures me that she sent them along to the Middling Way Kingdom, which both infuriates me and makes me sad that he won't even acknowledge us. Instead of dwelling on it, I try to enjoy each letter I receive from Sammi expressing her support and love. I miss her so much.

I don't allow myself to think of how much I miss that stupid troll.

CHAPTER 7

CAVEK

I don't know how long has passed. Many months, of that I am certain. From the dark cell, I cannot see the passage of seasons, but I track time by the daily ration of food they throw in at me. After the first several weeks, I began to feel like I was losing myself. Now I pace the cell like a caged beast. I even begin to look forward to my feeding time like a starving animal might.

My tormentors pay me a weekly visit whereupon they renew their punishment upon my body in attempt to extract what they want to know. All the while, I keep the image and memory of my female locked in the forefront of my mind to shut out everything afflicted upon me. I feel like I'll never be free of the stink of the male chosen to be my tormentor. I would like to forget about him in-between our sessions, but he makes that impossible.

Much to my dismay, he's also the one who is charged with feeding me. Krue leers at me from the other side of my cell as he holds up a particularly foul-looking piece of meat from his charcoal gray hand.

"Time to eat, troll. Come and get it. Not too sore from our playtime yesterday, are you?"

His grin widens as I approach the bars of my cell.

"I have to admit—I'm impressed. I never thought much of trolls. Certainly didn't think you'd survive as long as you have without cracking. What's your secret, I wonder?"

I narrow my eyes suspiciously. Krue is never this chatty.

"Do you have a female waiting for you at home? Is that it? It's funny how many males will suffer to survive to return to their mates. Is that what drives you to survive?"

I say nothing, closing my expression completely. The wolf is not fooled and lets out a bark of laughter.

"That *is* what it is. I knew it. Maybe I need to go find your female. I bet I can show her a much better time. Give her a little taste of what you've enjoyed all these months? Maybe I'll keep her. I need a female to breed my whelps. I can even do it in front of you when we finish our little sessions. I wonder if enough of your smell lingers on her that I can track her by that alone." He inhales deeply.

My gut clenches with anger and I react instantly, throwing myself against the bars with a howl of rage. Krue laughs like a maniac.

"You will not even think of touching my mate!"

"How do you think you'll stop me, all alone in your little cell?" he whispers as he leans forward. Much to my surprise, he suddenly freezes, his eyes widening.

"With aid of his kin," a deep voice growls from behind the werewolf as Serus plows into his side, knocking the large werewolf off his feet.

The keys to my cell clatter to the floor and are kicked toward our brother Garol, who enters just behind him. He has me free from my cell within seconds. I choose that moment to run as my brothers bid me as they dart out the door. I can hear a howl going up in the distance. The tribe has been alerted to their presence.

There's no time to delay.

I glance dispassionately down at Krue as he staggers to get up. He shakes his head as he lumbers to his feet, and his lips peel back from his fangs as he sees me lingering.

"I'm going to kill you!" he snarls seconds before he leaps at me.

Just as he's about to collide with me, I crouch and shove a dagger upward as I roll away. His scream rends the air around me as the blade buries to the hilt into his crotch, blood spurting with force from the severed major vein. I am covered in the male's blood as I rise to my feet.

A hand grips my arm roughly and I turn immediately ready to fight. I let out a breath and lower my hand as I see that it is only Serus. He'd returned when it became apparent that I was not right behind them.

"What is the matter with you?" he hisses. "We need to get out of here before the entire tribe's pack of warriors are upon us. They are only going to be distracted for so long before someone gets the idea to check on you."

He's right. We need to get out of here.

"Kate," I croak. It's the only word I can seem to force out.

Serus squeezes my shoulder. "We will find a way to get you to your mate, brother. Come on," he grunts as he flees into the shadows.

I follow in silence, my mind focused on only one thing: Kate.

Kate

I smile down at the tiny green hands of my son. He's a month old and growing fast. The dull black claws on each fingertip and toe are getting long enough to scratch me, and I know it's about time for another trim to shorten them to a manageable length and blunt the sharp edges.

I never would have guessed that a troll's claws would grow so fast.

"CJ," Boukie sings as she holds a brightly colored bear above him, rattling it. "Mister Bear is saying hello to you. Hello, CJ," she says in a gruff voice.

His dark purple eyes stare up at the bear hovering over his head, every so often turning toward his sister when she speaks, although it seems like a troll's vision as an infant is not much better than that of a human.

Cavek Junior, a name given when I failed to think of anything else to call a trollbie, is the same soft green of spring buds. He's a couple of shades darker than he was when he was born. He'd entered the world such a pale shade of green that at first, I had worried there was something wrong with him.

The midwife, upon hearing me voice my concern, assured me that trollbies tend to be light when they are born, but that he would get darker as he grew. Sure enough, two weeks later he was the color of new spring grass. Right now, his pastel coloring is a perfect complement to the little tuft of lavender hair that sits straight up from his brow like the small toys named after his species.

In short, he's adorable.

"Mommy, do you think Cavek will be surprised when he sees CJ?" Boukie innocently asks.

"I'm sure he will be," I murmur, playing along. When Cavek

never replied to the letter I sent about my pregnancy, I didn't bother to write to him again. I have no idea what he thinks about the baby. I do feel a little guilty for not writing after CJ was born. But the way I figure it, if he'd been interested, I would have heard back from him long before now. Still, it didn't hurt to play along.

"CJ is the prettiest brother in the whole world," Boukie coos, her fingers tickling the baby's round tummy. She leans forward, kisses his fat cheek, and whispers, "Don't worry, CJ. Your daddy is coming very soon. He's gonna take us and we are gonna be a prince and princess. We're gonna live in a big forest and be happy forever and ever."

"Boukie—"

"It's true, Mommy. Cavek promised. I dreamed of him. He's coming. He was in the dark but now he's coming for us. He won't leave us here. We're family. He's gonna be my daddy."

"Okay, baby," I concede, scooping CJ into my arms as he begins to squall, no longer satisfied with sucking on his little fist. I set him at my breast and smile down at him as his velvety purple eyes watch me as he suckles.

I have to admit, despite everything, I do wish that Cavek could see what we created between us. I wonder if he would be as instantly in love with him as I was when I first saw him.

∼

Cavek

"Cavek, this is foolish. You should be resting and allowing yourself more time to recover. Besides, it has been nearly a year. Maybe it would be better if you settle with a nice female here instead of traveling all the way to Ov'Ge. You have no idea what has happened between then and now," Father says, concern warring with disapproval on his face.

I understand his concern. Even weeks after finally returning home with my brothers, I am unwell. After two weeks of healing rest, it took three days of scrubbing my skin to even feel remotely clean again. But I do not feel whole. A vital part of me is missing that has been gone for nearly a year. I say as much and I am surprised to see a softening in my father's countenance.

"I think it is utterly romantic," Mother gushes. "After all this time, he is going after his female. You just don't have a romantic bone in your old grumpy body, Virol."

"You love this grumpy old unromantic body just fine," Father says with a grunt, making Mother giggle.

"It is a fine body," she agrees. "Our son deserves his own mate to shower love and admiration on him as well, so quit interfering."

"It is not that I am trying to interfere," he protests. He is doing exactly that. "I just don't want him to overtax himself and come to find out that he set his heart on disappointment."

"And how do you know she isn't waiting and pining for him?" Mother demands, setting her hands on her hips, her hair frizzing with the sudden surge of her temper.

"Ever since you took over the throne, you have been nothing but a grouch. You must remember what it was like when we were young, walking hand in hand around the lily ponds, making love under the pixie lights."

"Sampling each other's flesh throughout the night," Father says, his eyes brightening.

"Mother, Father, please!" I protest. The only thing worse than involuntarily imagining my siblings naked with their mates is imagining my parents having a sex life. Common sense says that they still enjoy each other. The way my mother likes to scream makes it hard to ignore that fact, but I absolutely don't need details.

"Very well, Cavek, if you insist. If Orgath allows you passage, you may retrieve your mate."

I don't even try to hold back my enthusiastic grin as I quickly bow and leave the throne room. I rush to my room and begin to pack a small bag in preparation to depart. I am in such a hurry to depart that I don't even notice my brother enter the room until he is standing beside me. Serus grins as he watches me.

"In a hurry?"

I glance up at him, wondering suspiciously at what his game is.

"As a matter of fact, I am," I say coolly.

"Going to Ov'Ge for your mate?"

"Yes."

"Splendid. I will come with you."

I falter and glance up at my brother. "Why would you do a thing like that?"

Serus shrugs. "Maybe I am bored."

"You have never been bored a day in your life. You can always find some sort of mischief to get into."

"True, but what better fun than to accompany my youngest brother to Ov'Ge? It should be quite entertaining watching you acquire your female."

My brows draw down into a scowl.

"You doubt me?"

He cannot contain his grin. "I doubt that your female will come as easily as you think she will."

"I never said I was going to ask."

That gives him pause. Serus stares at me for a long minute before slapping his leg and laughing loudly.

"Well then, you will definitely need me to make sure you don't get yourself or your female killed."

"Females," I correct.

"I beg your pardon?"

I sigh impatiently and narrow my eyes on my brother. "My mate has a small female child. Since she is my mate's daughter, she is now my daughter. We retrieve them both."

"Does Mother know you are providing her an instant grandchild?"

"No."

Serus rubs his hands together with glee. "An exceptional bonus. I can help you steal your mate and offspring *and* be present when Mother sees what you bring home."

"Don't you have a mate to tend to?"

"As it happens, she is away visiting family. I am all yours."

"Just great," I mutter.

"Isn't it?" he says jovially.

"Don't take this personally, but you're a pain in the ass. I hope Father rules for a very long time so that I don't have to deal with your ass on the throne."

To my surprise, Serus shudders. "Gods, let's hope so! I don't want it. What a perfectly miserable job. Of all of us, you are best suited to it. You seem to enjoy the misery of politics."

A snort of amusement escapes me, but in the end, I allow him to accompany me.

∼

It takes us less than two days' travel before we arrive at the orc chieftain's dwelling. It is not as grand as the troll palaces, nor as refined as those of the elves, yet it is sturdy and unshakeable like the orcs themselves. It is just as I remember it. I smile fondly and return the greetings of those orcs who remember me and shout their greetings.

"You are popular," Serus mutters.

"I am known. I helped their chieftain save his mate and overthrow the previous chieftain who was a bit of a bastard."

"Does Father know all of this?"

"To a degree."

"Minimal?"

"As much as possible," I admit with a small grin.

"Cavek, is that you?" a feminine voice calls down from a long staircase. I look up and see Sammi peering at me over the banister holding a young orc in her arms. Her eyes are wide with shock, and even I feel a bit startled. I know much time has passed during my captivity, but until now I hadn't truly considered just how much.

I missed so much.

I ignore my brother's obvious amusement and smile up at her.

"Of course. How many trolls do you personally know who'd just stroll into an orc chieftain's keep?"

Her laughter drifts down as she hurries down the stairs toward to me. "Not many, that is true. Oh, Cavek, where have you been!?"

"A bit of a misunderstanding with a werewolf tribe that had me forcibly detained for some time." Her mouth opens in surprise but I am quick to set her at ease. "But as you can see, I am whole and among the living."

"Were you given the letter that Kate sent for you?"

I frown down at her and exchange a look with my brother. He shrugs, just as clueless as I am.

"No, I did not. Kate sent me a letter?" My heart soars that she thought of me during the time we were apart.

Sammi clears her throat and glances around the room, hesitating before she speaks again.

"It really isn't my place to say anything... but it seemed important that she speak to you."

"That fits well with my plans. I am here to use the portal, with Orgath's permission," I add as the large male comes into view.

"Cavek," he says in greeting. "You are wishing entry into Ov'Ge?"

I straighten and face the orc with a stern expression as I would any opponent.

"I do."

"About fucking time," he says under his breath.

I ignore my brother's laughter. My day is already looking up.

CHAPTER 8

CAVEK

My only company through the portal this time is Serus, so I have to rely on my memory alone to get to Sammi's familial home. Orgath's mate did her best to refresh my memory after a years' absence had muddled so many details. I only hope that I understood her directions well and do not become lost.

A lost troll wandering around Anchorage wouldn't likely sit well with the local humans. Worse would be the months of laughter I would have to endure from my brother.

It would have been helpful if Sammi had come, as she had wanted, but Orgath refused out of concern for his mate's safety. I can certainly understand his position. With the mounting hostilities that humans demonstrated the last time they were in Ov'Ge, I'm not sure I would be comfortable with having my family here either.

Some species get away with it easier than others because they blend in better or are fairer in form. Orcs and trolls are not among them.

I smile with relief as we draw up to the narrow path leading up to the door of the exact building I was looking for. A crash behind me makes me freeze until my brother's low curses cut through the air. The smell of refuse that follows makes me laugh for the first time in months.

"What the fucking hell is this?" Serus asks.

"It must be trash night," I observe. I recall Jake telling me of this weekly ritual. "You tripped over a refuse bin."

"Humans put waste in bins? That is disgusting. Blessed gods, what is this white rolled up thing? It is putrid!" I turn to look back at him when he sputters and flings it away in disgust. "That thing was covered in shit! Gods of the abyss, I have it all over me."

Assuming that he must be exaggerating or causing an unnecessary fuss, I turn around and approach him. I notice the foul stench seconds before I see the source. A foot away from Serus, an infant butt-covering lies open on the ground covered in the most repulsive green shit I have ever seen. Glancing at my brother, still muttering as he rises to his feet, confirms that his entire left thigh is covered in the mess.

"You never said that humans are this disgusting."

"That belongs to a newly-born offspring, I would guess. Such things are by nature disgusting."

"Now I smell as foul as a trollbie," he grouses darkly.

"Just smell like it as far away from me as possible," I mutter, earning a disgusted look from my sibling.

I frown at the house. I don't recall there being anyone here who would have a baby. Perhaps Luke has mated and producing young? Not that it matters. I'm here to find out where my mate is and be on my way. Unless this is the wrong house... but I don't think so. My nostrils flare and I detect the scents of Lucy, Luke, and David, all strong enough to indicate they're at home. I don't have a nose like a werewolf or some other creatures of Ov'Gorg, but it's strong enough to detect familiar bodies.

I pause and my heart beats stronger as I catch the rich scent of my female and Boukie. And a third. A male, who is oddly at once both familiar but a complete stranger to my senses.

My family is here with another male.

Anger rushes through me that cannot be contained or reasoned with. Father had attempted to prepare me for this possibility, but I do not care. I will destroy any male who attempts to get between me and my mate.

"Cavek, what is it?" Serus shouts as I run toward the front door of the house.

I do not bother answering him. To do so serves no purpose. I'm consumed by the knowledge that another male is in my place. It is unbearable. An honorable male would cede to his rival, but months in a dank werewolf's cell killed that part of me.

I refuse to give up the one thing that kept me going.

I can feel Serus behind me as I insert the flat of a blade between the door and its frame and effortlessly pry it open.

"These humans do not have much in the way of security," Serus observes quietly as he slips inside following close behind me. I know without even looking that he is attempting to examine everything at once as we go through the house as I track my female's scent.

I make my way soundlessly through the house until I arrive first at the room I shared with Ferli and Bodi. The scent of Boukie comes strongly from this room. I will retrieve my human offspring.

I ease the door open and creep inside. A smile spreads over my face when I catch sight of a small slender arm thrown over a pillow and a tiny foot hanging from the coverings on the bed. I gently peel back the covering, revealing Boukie's flushed face buried against the pillow.

"This is your mate's offspring? She is very small," Serus whispers.

I spare him a nod, but my attention is on the little female. She's grown so much in the time I have been gone that it makes my heart ache. Boukie stirs and open her eyes, blinking against her fatigue. Her eyes widen suddenly, and she shoots up in her bed.

"Cavek!" she shrieks, springing into my arms.

I quickly hush her, but I can't hold back my happiness as I enfold her in my arms.

"You're here! I told Mommy," she whispers fiercely, making my heart swell with love. "You didn't forget us."

"I would never forget you," I whisper, my heart in my throat.

I motion to my brother, who slowly approaches. Boukie's eyes widen further, taking in his massive size.

"This is my brother, Serus. He's come all this way to help me bring you home."

Serus outstretches a hand and, after a moment, she trustingly sets her own hand in his grasp.

"Greetings, Boukie," Serus whispers.

"Hi, Uncle Serus," she returns.

The effect is devastating on my brother. His face softens and he bestows a broad smile upon her. As usual, Boukie is not even deterred by his large fangs. She reaches up and grasps his face between her hands in wonder before dragging his head down to wrap her arms around his neck and hug him.

"Serus is going to carry you, okay?"

"Okay," she whispers.

"I am going to get your mommy now."

"Don't forget CJ," she says, her voice rising slightly as I frantically wave her down.

I can't help but fume as questions stir within me. Who is this CJ to my females? Was my daughter attached to this male already? Surely Boukie would not expect me to bring him with me.

"Where is CJ?" I ask, trying to keep the growl out of my voice.

"He sleeps with Mommy. We have to take him with us."

Everything within me rebels at the mere suggestion. I thrust my mounting anger aside. I am certainly not taking this male with us. But I can kill this CJ later, I decide. My first priority is retrieving my mate.

Serus respectfully waits outside the door as I slip into her room. My heart stops as I spy her form sleeping alone curled up under the blanket, her mass of dark hair fanned out over the pillow. I don't see the male anywhere. It's possible I can remove her before he even notices she's missing.

I pull back the blanket, exposing her delectable form covered with nothing more than an oversized tunic decorated with the outline of a giant bat across her breasts. I inhale deeply, feeling peace for the first time in so long.

I have dreamed of this moment.

Summoning the magic from within my belly, I lean forward and exhale over her. The pale pink smoke ignited within me issues out from my lungs and surrounds her, drawing into her body as she breathes it in. I relax, this part of my task complete. The breath of sleep will keep her slumbering for many hours.

My eyes wander down further and then stop. Everything within me freezes as I stare at a small form curled against my mate's belly. The little one is clad in a long bit of cloth gathered beneath its feet, but the pale green skin and the tuft of lavender hair are that of a healthy trollbie.

I draw the tiny male's scent deep into my lungs, savoring it, imprinting it upon my being. This is my son. The urge to weep sweeps over me like a sudden riptide. All the pain and suffering I went through, all that I missed—my female round with our young and the birth of my son—everything is worth this very moment.

"Cavek, what is taking so long?" Serus whispers loud enough to carry.

I don't want to relinquish my son, but I need my hands free to transport Kate and it will be easier to do if she's not awake. I retreat back through the door, wrapping my son in a blanket I pulled off the back of a strange chair that glides on its base. Serus cranes his head to see what I am holding bundled in my arms but suddenly growls and whips around with his sword ready at a sound coming up behind us. I still, prepared to defend my mate and offspring.

"Cavek, is that you?" a male's voice echoes down the hallway.

I relax, recognition flooding me at the familiar scent and sound of his voice.

"Luke," I greet the male as he comes around the corner, pushing my brother's hand and weapon aside. "I have returned for my family."

Luke squints up at me, brushing back the locks of his hair covering his eyes. After a few more nervous glances at my brother, he nods.

"I figured you might eventually. But I didn't think it would take you so long," he finishes with a disapproving frown.

"Are you questioning my brother's honor?" Serus steps forward and snarls with menace.

My brother is a complete dick, but I can count on him to have my back in almost any situation.

"It's okay, Serus," I say. "It is a fair observation. I don't blame the male for questioning me." I turn my attention fully on Luke. "I intended to return within days but ended up caged by my enemies for a number of months until my brothers could free me."

Luke pales.

"This place you're taking them... is it safe?"

I cock my head and regard the human.

"Is any place truly safe? Can you guarantee we would be safe here? Would my son be safe maturing here?"

I can feel the weight of Serus's gaze and feel him shift behind me. His confusion is nigh palpable.

Luke considers my point for minute then shakes his head with a wan smile.

"No, I suppose not."

"Help me then. Help me get my family to the portal."

"You aren't going to wake Kate first?" Luke asks, a frown once more pulling at his lips.

I refrain from answering, knowing that the male will not care for it but I do not feel concerned with it either way. He may consider Kate his family, but he's not her mate nor her father. He has zero authority over me where it concerns her.

"Awake, she is guaranteed to draw the unwanted attention of our enemies to us as we pass through Ov'Gorg to our territory. I plan on placing sleep on my children as well. We will wrap them in swathes of cloth as if transporting goods back from the orc village and none will be the wiser."

Luke narrows his eyes at me.

"I don't like that you're doing this without her knowing. It's not right."

"Are you planning on stopping me?" I growl, no longer interested in mincing words with this human.

Being a smart male, Luke blows out a breath and concedes. "Yeah, okay. Look, I can take you in her car wherever you need to go. Just give me a minute to find my shoes and her car keys. Kate's going to fucking kill me," he says as he walks away.

I face my brother just as Serus draws up to my side and looks speculatively down at the bundle in my arms. By some chance, my son chooses that moment to turn in my arms and exposes his little face as he shoves the blanket away from his body. My brother's breath hitches in wonder.

"Cavek, is that...?"

"My son," I say, my voice choked around a sudden blockage in my throat.

"That's CJ," Boukie explains.

Serus reaches a claw-tipped finger toward him in wonder as CJ opens his mouth in a wide yawn. My brother chuckles.

"He certainly looks just like you," he observes. He leans forward and sniffs at the child's head. "Even smells a little like you. I am surprised neither one of us caught that until now." A wide grin suddenly splits his face. "This is great news! This is guaranteed to give me a few years respite from Mother hounding me to provide her with grandchildren. Maybe by then you will have spawned another."

I grunt at my brother's hilarity as Luke returns with a strange sort of hard basket.

"What is that?"

Luke doesn't reply but gestures for me to hand him CJ. I hold him tighter, my refusal clear. The human sighs.

"This is an infant car seat. CJ has to be strapped into this anytime we travel. To keep him safe."

I eye the contraption with suspicion. It does seem like it would provide adequate support for my offspring with its thick padding, and I really can't argue if it is a safety device...

"I don't like it. I would rather not be separated from my son," I say, drawing my son closer to my chest with a rumble.

Luke runs his hand down in his face in an obvious show of exasperation, but I don't care.

"Cavek, I can't drive around with you holding him. Not only is it really dangerous if we get into an accident, it's against the law."

"You would think he'd be more worried about getting on the

wrong side of a troll," Serus mutters, making my lips twitch upward.

I knock aside Luke's arms and place my offspring in the contraption. The buckles are simple to figure out as I secure my young into the seat. I pull back and marvel at it. Although I hate the separation, it does seem quite useful.

I accompany Luke to the car and observe as he secures the car seat into a flat base while Boukie climbs into her seat and instructs Serus on how to "buckle her in." My brother snarls as the strap gets stuck twice in its descent before finally pulling the rest of the way down to secure my daughter.

When I return with Kate, Serus is folded into the seat beside Boukie, leaving the other seat in front free for me to occupy with my mate in my arms. The fit is cramped, and Luke takes one look at all of us and lets loose a litany of foul words with the proclamation that we were 'nothing but an accident waiting to happen.' The way he speaks, I'm certain there are road guards waiting to apprehend us the moment we begin to travel. But by some miracle, we arrive at our destination without incident.

In spite of his impatience, Luke hugs my offspring to him with a certain sadness in his eyes and lingers to watch as we proceed through the portal.

That's a male who could use a nice troll female to teach him how to enjoy life.

Maybe I will get Mother on it.

CHAPTER 9

KATE

I stretch leisurely. That had to have been, without a doubt, one of the best nights of sleep I've gotten in over a month. Maybe even longer. Yawning, I blink up at the soft glow of the golden lights overhead. A ceiling of delicately woven root systems runs smoothly toward the walls, where they continue in their course to disappear into the floor.

That's... different.

My eyes dart over the room, and I resist the urge to vomit as the world shifts around me. The pulse of a migraine beats behind my eyes but I attempt to ignore it as I take in the environment around me.

Nothing is familiar. It's like I was plucked up from my own bed and dropped into this room, wherever I am. The random brilliant hues in the fabrics and plush pillows are almost overwhelming. Even the bed feels extraordinarily lush.

Wait. Something is missing. No, someone.

I slide my hand over to run my fingers along the bedding at

THE TROLL BRIDE

my side, hunting for CJ. Panic wells inside me as I realize the space beside me is completely empty. I throw the blankets back and sit up with an alarmed shriek, my head whipping around.

"Kate—"

In a mode of instinctual self-preservation, I turn and strike up with the heel of my hand only seconds before registering the owner of the voice. Cavek yelps and shields his face with his hands, his eyes watering.

"Damnation of the gods, Kate. What was that for?"

"Cavek? Is that really you? I'm not hallucinating or something?"

He lowers his hands and he scrunches up his nose as if testing the damage before flashing what he seems to think is a charming fang-filled smile. Leaning forward, he takes my hand in his and looks me in the eyes, the swirls of purple shifting in his orbs.

"Do not worry, Kate. You are now home."

"I'm home? Well, that just leaves me with one question," I whisper, drawing him closer to me.

His eyes brighten and his voice drops into a seductive purr that I have zero resistance against. Squishing my thighs together, I desperately try to ignore it as he leans in.

"What is that?" he murmurs.

My lips curve in what he obviously thinks is a seductive smile as I press my breasts against him. One of my hands trails along his shoulder while the other fumbles through the bedding until it finds a pillow, and I smack him right in the face with it.

"Where the hell are my children, Cavek?" I shout as I proceed to whack him with the plush citrine-colored weapon.

"Wait, wait, Kate... oww, damnit, that caught me in the nose... they're here."

My hand halts in mid-strike, leaving a vulnerable opening that Cavek takes advantage of. Throwing himself across my body, Cavek pins me to the bed as he yanks the pillow from my grip and tosses it across the room. His lavender hair threads around his head in a chaotic mess and his eyes narrow on me like laser beams.

"Where. Are. They," I grit out.

"In the common room with my brother Serus. Did you really have to hit me like that?"

"Uh, yeah. I wake up in a strange place... my head throbbing by the way, what the fuck did you drug me with? I feel like I'm suffering from the worst hangover ever... and my children are gone. Of course I'm going to strike first and ask questions second. What the hell did you think you were doing bringing me here without waking me up first?"

"I wanted to. Okay, no, that's a lie. I was dreading this moment so I wasn't eager to wake you, but I couldn't risk any of you being awake while we traveled through enemy territory. I don't know what would have happened if I had been spotted returning with you rather than what looked like lumps of traded goods. I cannot risk you. Any of you."

I stare at him, digesting everything he said and turning every possible scenario over in my head of something else he could have done.

"You could have at least woken me up and explained all of that to me."

He nodded. "You are right. I wasn't ready. I will not lie and say I regret it, but I am sorry if you feel hurt or angered by my decision. Still, I think the result would have been the same. A trollbie will never be accepted in Ov'Ge as things stand right now."

I let out a breath. "I understand. I'm sorry I tried to break your nose. I may have overreacted."

"You think so?"

"Not that you wouldn't have deserved it. But truthfully, I didn't recognize you. Don't you know better than to sneak up on

THE TROLL BRIDE

someone while they're waking up?" I pause thoughtfully. "So, they are safe with your brother?"

Cavek immediately looks insulted.

"Of course they are. They are with my brother, heir of the Troll Kingdom of the Middling Way. More importantly, they are with family. He would protect them with his life."

My muscles start to relax but as my anxiety decreases, my questions increase. As does my anger.

"I'm glad that you finally got to meet CJ," I say in a whisper.

The blissfully happy smile that spreads across his face stops me in my tracks. I wasn't expecting my eventual confrontation with Cavek going this way. He's far too happy for a male who ignored my letter and expressed zero interest in the baby he fathered.

"I'm very happy to have him. He has my heart already." He pauses and a slight frown mars his brow. "I have missed so much. I didn't get to be there to greet him in the troll custom. I should have been there at his naming to present him before the ancestors and the spirits of our forest. Still, you did well, Kate. He is healthy and a fine trollbie. Ceeja is a strange name, but it sounds strong. I approve."

"You should. CJ is named after you."

Confusion pulls at his brow. "I don't understand."

"When we name a baby boy after his father, we add the prefix 'Junior.' CJ is short for Cavek Junior. I couldn't think of a better name for him."

His face brightens with wonder and I can't help the flush of pleasure I feel at that.

"My Cavekji," he says with obvious pride, speaking to absolutely no one but himself. I wonder for a minute if he's forgotten I'm even in the room. I clear my throat.

"I'm honestly surprised you're interested. You never replied to the letter I sent, and you never came back."

I'm taken aback when Cavek leaps to his feet and begins to stalk in a high-powered pace, agitation showing in every bunch of his muscles. He draws one hand through his hair, the other clenching and unclenching at his side. He says nothing for several minutes but then surprises me by kneeling in front of me, his thick fingers gripping my thighs. His head lies across my lap and my breath stops at this sudden show of vulnerability.

"My apologies, Kate. I don't know what happened to the letter, but I swear by the gods, my ancestors, and the spirit keepers of this wood that I would never have left you and our family in Ov'Ge without a word. I always intended to come back for you." He chokes with feeling as if he's forcing out the words painfully from within him. All the anger I've built up begins to crumble in that moment.

"What happened? When you left, I thought you were going to come back—at least once," I whisper, baring all my sadness before him.

His arms wrap tightly around my legs and a shudder wracks his body.

"I meant to. By the gods, I meant to return to you just a handful of days after I left. My father demanded I aid Serus in an issue with our borders, but I was captured by the northern werewolf tribe."

"Werewolves?" My disbelief is plain in my tone. "Men who are cursed to change into wolves with the full moon... Really, that's the story you're going with?"

Cavek's head jerks up, his eyes flashing.

"No, Kate. Werewolves may sometimes take the form of men, but they are something that is neither man nor wolf. Tall as the largest troll, rivaling an orc in height, they're lethal creatures who have territories that border our woods. They captured me. For a year, they tortured me in the worst ways they could think of until there wasn't a place upon me that didn't hurt from their torment."

My mouth goes dry and I stare at his flat expression.

"What happened?" I manage to croak.

He shakes his head, and a scant, wry smile curves his lips before disappearing again. His fingers absently trace patterns on the back of my hands.

"Wards to alert you against danger," he whispers, answering my unspoken question.

He kisses my palms with a sigh.

"My brothers liberated me and got me home. I swear to you, Kate: I came for you as soon as I recovered from my ordeal. Sooner than the healers and my kin liked. But I couldn't leave you and Boukie in Ov'Ge a moment longer. And I'm glad that I disobeyed, because that brought Cavekji to me."

For the first time, I notice the interlacing scars that mar his beautiful emerald skin. I can't see all of them, since he's wearing his loose breeches, but I'm horrified to think what damage was done to him as I observe the scars disappearing into the waist of his pants. I inhale and blow out a long breath, willing myself to release the feelings that had grown toxic within me.

"How did you get us here without waking me?"

His grin is so sheepish that it takes everything not to laugh.

"About that. Trolls have a magic called the breath of sleep. It's a powerful sedative that will make whomever we breathe it upon sleep for a number of hours. Luke helped transport you and our offspring to the portal. Sammi and Orgath aided us in transporting you the rest of the way. I kept Cavekji with you as much as possible so that he could feed while you slept. It worked wonderfully."

"Did they really?" I ask, totally focused on my family's collaboration with my disappearance, although I felt no small amount of relief that someone had the sense to help CJ nurse while I was out of it.

"Only because I didn't expect Cavekji and don't possess

enough arms to carry both of you," he amends in a rush. Despite his words, I can tell he isn't cowed by my displeasure in the least. His face flattens into the familiar stubborn, ruthless lines I remember so well.

"Regardless, you are mine, as are Boukie and Cavekji," he continues, his tone firm. "The troll kingdom is the best place for our family, and I am sure you understand why. We will dwell in my den on my ancestral territory and live our lives together as the gods intend."

I want to snap back at him, but I'm honestly so damned relieved to have someone take a major decision out of my hands that I have no interest in fighting him on it. It's exhausting being the only one who has to make all the decisions over every minuscule thing. He wants to be in charge? He can have it. That doesn't mean I'll always agree with him, but it's a good place to start.

Not that I'm going to make life easy on him.

I incline my head in acknowledgment and he seems surprised, but then complete masculine satisfaction spreads over his face. He leans forward and caresses his soft, full lips against my own, sucking and nibbling on my lower lip until I'm practically panting against his mouth before he pulls away at long last.

"I suppose you wish to see our offspring," he teases.

At this moment, my children are the furthest thing from my mind and by his tone I know that he knows it. I chuckle and shove at the strong arm that still cages me in.

"Yes, take me to our children, you brute."

With a great show of reluctance, he pushes himself off the bed, one hand lingering just long enough to grab my hand and yank me to my feet. I'm propelled out the door and down a short hallway until I step into a cozy room lit with a warm fire and several golden lights hanging in the air, just like the ones in the bedroom. Since I wasn't able to look at them close-up, I take a moment to stare and marvel at their golden shimmer before my attention is promptly snared by my daughter's antics.

A giant troll sits on a plush high-backed chair, one arm extended away from his body as Boukie climbs him like a monkey, the other arm curved protectively around a soundly sleeping CJ. He's so massive my first impulse is to rip my children away from him and demand to know who he is. But that would be silly since Cavek just told me that his brother was minding them. This guy must be Serus. At that moment, the male spies me and bares an alarmingly massive set of sharp teeth as he smiles politely at Cavek's introduction.

I forcibly unglue my tongue from the roof of my mouth and offer a polite greeting as Boukie lets out another squeal and wraps her arms around Serus's thick neck. He gingerly hand CJ to his father and sweeps Boukie around as if providing her with a private jungle gym on his form. As I watch them, my alarm slowly fades, and I can't help but feel moved by the sight of them together.

Cavek is a rotten bastard for the way he got us here, but there's no doubt in my mind this is probably the best place for us.

Boukie, as wild and impulsive as she is, can thrive here without recrimination if Serus is anything to go by. I doubt I'll have the stream of endless complaints from her instructors as I had the last year from her teacher. And CJ will be able to enjoy a normal childhood like any other troll. I'm not sure what this will mean for me, but I find that part of me is actually excited to find out. I'm suddenly living my favorite fantasy with a guy who stirs my blood like no other, one who also not only fathered my son but accepts my daughter as his own with full paternal devotion.

I really can't think of anything more that I want at this moment.

Except maybe love, an insidious voice whispers in the back of my mind, but I tell it to shut up. This is enough for now.

CHAPTER 10

KATE

This world is like nothing I ever imagined, not even with the descriptions Sammi gave over the months through our regular correspondence. The landscape itself is quite different. There are no high mountains, except those barely visible in the far distance, nor are there stretches of grassy plains.

Instead, everywhere I look there are massive, thick trees reaching up to weave their branches into a near-impenetrable canopy. The light filtering down is muted but several species of plants and flowers have a fascinating bioluminescence that provide a source of light along the trails of the forest. Everywhere there are countless springs that feed into larger swamps that Cavek points out at a distance.

"Are there alligators there?" Boukie asks, completely captivated, as we cross over a bridge under which a murky river flows into the swamp.

"I don't believe I have ever heard of any such thing," Cavek chuckles as he leans slightly into me, his body brushing along mine. "But there are a number of beings and creatures who call the swamps their home. Some of them are quite dangerous, and they will swallow you up if you give into the slumber-inducing vapors released in the depths of the swamp by the nightbloom swamp lilies."

I watch with rapt fascination as a flurry of lights chases each other over the green-tinged water flush with flora.

"Are those fireflies?" I ask with interest. Although I had spent some time outside of Alaska, I hadn't seen fireflies before.

Cavek looks in the direction I'm pointing and smiles.

"Pixies," he announces as if speaking of something as common as a honeybee rather than a magnificent being of any girl's childhood fantasies. "They are among some of the most skilled weavers. They work their own spun silks to make some of the finest garments." He watches quietly as they disperse. "It appears they just left the castle."

A strangler appears in front of us, a dainty female about the size of my hand with small, bare breasts and a flare of hips off which tiny ribbons flow behind her as her only form of covering. Her small body shimmers, radiating with a rosy light as if burning from a fire lit at the core of her body, where the light is the brightest. She flits in the air in front of us like a hummingbird as she sketches a quick bow before darting off after her brethren.

My awe at the moment is overshadowed as I spot the towering palace rise up between the trees, resembling a mass of gnarled roots solidified together and overflowing with lush green life. It's so magnificent that at first, I'm uncertain if it's real or if I had stepped into a beautifully painted fantasy landscape. I've never seen colors so lush and vivid despite the long shadows of the woods. A heavy palette of lavender, silver, and rose hues amid sparkling ruby and amethyst would be the obvious favorite of any artist who attempts to capture this sight.

I swallow nervously and wish we were back in Cavek's

comfortable den in the heavy roots of the ancient tree. I shouldn't have let him talk me into this. I only just arrived this morning. Summons from the palace be damned. After all, I'm still trying to get used to being in Ov'Gorg, much less the Middling Way Kingdom. The idea of meeting the queen—and my lover's mother—is rather terrifying. I clutch CJ closer to me, his tiny body wriggling in protest even in his slumber.

Cavek seems to notice because he frowns at me with concern.

"Do not worry. Everything will be fine. My mother is very eager to meet you."

I find that hard to believe, but Serus decides to back him up.

"What Cavek says is true," he airily agrees from just behind us where Boukie comfortably sits on his shoulders surveying our new home. "Mother has been waiting many years for the day Cavek brings home a female. She has been quite vocal."

"Nagging, launching into inspirational song, arranging for theatrical performances on the grandeur of love, sometimes downright threatening," Cavek says with a shudder.

Serus grins at his brother, clearly amused by his discomfort.

"Do not worry, Kate. I assure you she is quite happy," Serus finishes with a satisfied melodic hum.

I nearly jump out of my skin when the heavily armed guards at either side of the entrance step forward. At first, I think they mean to attack, but they bow instead and step aside, allowing us to pass.

Inside, the halls are lit with sconces filled with a sort of mystic blue fire. I'm not sure how much the trolls need that light as I observe Cavek and Serus's eyes illuminate with an eerie glow, but I'm grateful for them or else I would be stumbling around the palace near-blind in the dim, natural light. Despite their attempts at offering comforting and reassuring words, my apprehension doesn't let up even a little as Cavek steers into the throne room.

THE TROLL BRIDE

To my relief, the throne room appears empty when we arrive. This is short-lived when suddenly a large, plump female of a brilliant hue of green with wild, dark lavender hair pops up in front of us, a horrifying shriek issuing from her wide, smiling mouth. That obviously friendly smile is the only thing that doesn't have me bolting for the door. That, and Cavek's iron grip on my arm.

"You are *here*," she trills as her thick arms wrap around me and she hugs me to her large bosom. The clouds of bright pink silk pool around her with her movements and obscure most of my vision. The contrast between her coloring and the silk is if someone took a lime-green gummy bear and dipped it in Pepto-Bismol. CJ whimpers in between us and she sets me down with a rapt look of fawning adoration.

"A trollbie!" she exclaims, relieving me of my son before my brain catches up to what she intended to do. She hugs him to her, almost shaking with happiness. "Finally, a baby in the palace again. All these years I've been telling my children that I need babies in the palace. I'm not getting any younger. But do you think any of them listen to me? Of course not. You'd think I was asking them to throw themselves into the swamp with stones in their pockets if I so much as mention mates and trollbies," she says with a firm shake of her head. "He is so precious. What did you name him?"

"Cavekji," I say slowly, hoping that I am pronouncing the troll variation of his name correctly. By the way Cavek's lips tilt up with pride, I'm guessing that I nailed it.

"Oh, what a perfect name!" She levels Serus with a hard look. "See? How hard is it, Serus, for you to provide me with a trollbie? Your brother was only with Kate once and managed to make a beautiful son and acquire a daughter. Hello, dear little Boukie. What a fine trollbie you will make. Where are all of *your* children, Serus? You and your mate have had plenty of time."

Her face brightens as she turns to address me again. "Where

are my manners? I am Madi, but Mother suits me better. I am so very happy Cavek has found a mate at last! But you are too small. You must eat more."

The queen is nothing short of a living whirlwind. I stare at her with the kind of awestruck shock that someone feels watching a four-car pile-up on the highway. It's all I can even think to do. I work my mouth wordlessly as she breezes by, heading out the room *with my babies*. CJ is in one arm, and she holds Boukie's hand as my daughter chatters up at her.

"I dreamed Cavek came," Boukie announces as she looks up, enthralled with Madi. I can tell even from a distance that the female looks suitably impressed.

"Is that so!"

It's hard to tell if Madi is saying that for Boukie's benefit or if she's being earnest, but my little girl beams with pleasure.

"I did. I always, always dreamed he came."

"Well, that is something very special," Madi praised, but I lost the rest of the conversation as Cavek drew me back beside him and nuzzled my neck affectionately. Heat fills me so suddenly I'm surprised that my bones don't start melting on the spot.

"Don't worry about the trollbies!" she suddenly yells without even looking back at us. "I have them well in hand. You two go spend some time together and... reconnect. I will bring the children by in a little while." I can almost hear the pleased smile in her voice.

"Cavek, make sure she gets plenty to eat," she adds. "You are a large troll and we don't want you breaking her when inspired with your male lusts."

Serus chuckles and gives Cavek a playful nudge with his shoulder as he passes, trailing behind the queen.

"Yes, do be careful of those male lusts, brother," he taunts.

"Well," I say slowly, stifling a giggle, "that meeting was ... something."

I feel Cavek laugh against my skin.

"I fear that Mother gets a little overexcited at times and has a very strong opinion on everything, even if she wields it in a manner that can embarrass her children from time to time."

Now that I have had a moment to absorb what happened, I find myself smiling. I can't help but like the overt honesty of the queen. There's nothing demure, quiet or even anything in the range of what humans consider polite. It's refreshing. She obviously absolutely adores both children, despite Boukie not being of any blood relation.

"I think that's great, even if it's a bit overwhelming. I didn't think she would embrace Boukie so quickly," I admit.

Cavek raises one thick lavender eyebrow and his lips curl.

"Trolls are not quite as xenophobic as some species. We easily adopt offspring into our families. Those we adopt are no different in our eyes than any other trollbie and are just as loved. As far as Mother is concerned, Boukie is just another trollbie she can spoil," he says with a laugh. "Do not worry. I doubt she will even put Cavekji down the entire time we are gone, nor will Boukie set foot out of her sight."

I am a bit concerned, but between Madi's enthusiasm and Cavek's endorsement I feel a little better about the idea of leaving my children with her for some adult time. In any case, there's obviously a palace full of guards and servants on hand if my children need anything at all. I never thought I would be the kind of person who had servants around, but this goes a long way to allay my fears of having my children out of my sight for even a short time.

My mouth dries as the humor in Cavek's eyes dies down almost as quickly as it sprung, and it is replaced with a scorching heat just seconds before his lips crash down upon my own. My senses reel and I feel completely off-kilter as I'm suffused with the scent and taste of him. When he finally pulls away, I have to grip his arm to steady myself, my breath coming out in ragged pants.

"What was that?" I whisper a bit louder than I intended.

He grins down at me, his eyes sparkling playfully.

"That was just a taste of what is in store for you. But first, come, Kate. Let's abscond to our home and dine in what privacy we can find together for this little time that we have alone."

Even though a blush spreads across my cheeks at the suggestion, I'm totally on board. My libido, silent for a year, suddenly roars to life with keen interest.

Yes, I can definitely use some private time with Cavek before the mommy duties return.

"Well, what are we waiting for? Onward home," I say, my lips curving enticingly. His guttural growl lets me know the feeling is mutual. I'm almost quaking with excitement as we follow the path that leads to Cavek's den.

CHAPTER 11

KATE

My hand rests in Cavek's as he leads me in the approximate direction of his home, but we follow a different network of paths that seems a bit less direct than the scenic swamp route we took to get to the palace. This time, he leads me into the darker depths of the forest where the ethereal glow from the luminous vine and flowers are the only source of light. The little motes of pollen drift on the breeze, gleaming as they up the light every now and again.

I can't deny it's pretty romantic.

He leads me onto a bridge. Just below me, I see a shimmering pond thick with lotus blooms, brimming with a pale purple light at their centers that shines through the translucent petals. Pixies skip over the lotuses like dragonflies, their wings creating a soft singing hum in the air.

Cavek leans forward and whispers, "The pixies consume nectar much like bees. I have heard that in most ancient times in Ov'Ge, some called them nymphai and said it was due to how they hover over water like bees. Of all the flowers, they prefer that of the immortal lotus."

"That's amazing," I reply in a hushed tone, not wishing to disturb the industry of the pixies. Some of them stop to chase playfully after each other before resuming their task.

"Do they live in hives like bees?"

"Not hives exactly, but they build complex networks high in the trees in various hollows. Pixies have a rather complicated social system. They are matriarchal, the females being larger and brighter than the smaller male pixies who keep the nests and protect them in their larger numbers. You can always spot a mated pixie because she never goes anywhere without the escort of her mates. Ah, there are some males there, accompanying their female."

I lean into him, relishing the warmth and scent of his body as I look to where he points and see four smaller blue and white lights dance protectively around the larger brilliant orange light of a female pixie as she gathers the nectar.

"They're guarding her while she works," I observe, enthralled.

I watch their lights flicker and bounce as they move around her like a tiny swarm as their female moves from one flower to another.

"Why do their lights flicker while her light remains constant?"

Cavek's hands skate down my belly, making heat curl and bloom inside of me. He breathes into my ear as he murmurs.

"To warn off other males and to demonstrate to predators that they will defend her. The faster a male's light blinks the stronger he is. On the longest day of the year, the males come to this pond and try to attract a queen for their nest, demonstrating in shows of flickering lights to impress the females."

His lips trail down from my ear and lightly kiss my neck, making my toes curl.

"Will you bring me to see it?" I breathe, my voice already shaking with need.

Cavek chuckles. "Of course. It isn't proper for a child to witness the pixie orgies as the females accept their males, but adult trolls will often find secluded lotus patches near their own homes to enjoy the aphrodisiac effect of the pixie dust. We will be sure to do this."

My lips part with surprise. Who knew that something as seemingly innocent as pixies would be so X-rated? And who knew I would be so deviant as to be completely turned on by the idea of rolling in the grass with Cavek under the influence of pixie dust orgies?

His lips unerringly find mine, and their sweet caress is just as I remember—but even better. I shudder. I can't believe the words that are about to come out of my mouth.

"Cavek, maybe we should slow down a bit. We rushed into things when we met, but it might be a good idea to take our time getting to know each other. Just give it a couple of days at least. We owe it to our children to work on building our relationship outside of great sex."

"Well, great sex was a good place to start," Cavek says with a smutty grin that makes me laugh. He runs his hand through his hair and sighs, guilt flashing on his features. "You are right, Kate. I want to court you the proper way a troll courts his female. We didn't get that opportunity."

He pauses and looks at me thoughtfully. "By tradition you would live with your mother until our courting finishes, but I don't think I would survive being separated from you and the little ones. Although, we should find a ceremonial fostering family for you."

I arch an eyebrow. "Ceremonial fostering family?"

He nods. "According to troll mating traditions, the females and males compete in contests of strength and agility, usually via fighting and dancing, to prove their worth to join their lines together."

I stare at him in shock. I'm not sure what surprises me more. The barbaric traditions—actually, that doesn't really surprise me since we're talking about trolls—or the fact that Cavek is already talking of mating in the same breath as courting. Like the future is already written.

Is it just because of CJ? Although he has much to do with where we are finding ourselves now and trying to build a relationship, I don't want someone to tie themselves to me just because of CJ. I want something real to build between us before we consider something that serious. He seems to note the aghast look on my face because he switches gears quickly.

"Come along, Kate. We're nearly home. I am sure you must be hungry."

I murmur an agreement as we continue across the bridge and follow the path around to the den.

∽

Cavek

Kate stands beside me, silently helping me as we work together to prepare the evening meal. I had to instruct her with a few things that she is unfamiliar with, but the easy companionship is comfortable. Still, frustration twists in my gut.

It is important to court her and develop our bonds, but I am frustrated that she doesn't understand the ties between us. Orgath explained some of the frustration with being mated to a human, and high on that list is that they do not sense these things as denizens of Ov'Gorg do. Not all species have bloodbonded mates, but it's common among the races of elves, trolls, and orcs, likely due to our close relation to each other. Other races have their own ways to identify a suitable mate without much difficulty when they find the right one.

Among trolls, if we recognize our bloodbond we know, even through the courting period, it will eventually culminate in our mating. It is a near-certain thing, something celebrated by both families through the entire process. The courting is merely the essential bonding period. Of course, trolls still possess free will. We can choose not to bond or mate with our bloodbond, but few are willing to go that route.

We sit together at the low orcish-style table that many trolls prefer. The craftsmanship of finely hewn orc tables is unparallel to most things outside of gem-inlaid stone tables crafted by dwarves. Although we have artisans among us, few trolls have the patience to meticulously craft such items as furniture, but we are happy to trade wood from our forests to make things for our pleasure.

"This is a lovely table," Kate remarks, running a hand along its surface, her fingers tracing the delicately carved flowers and knotted trees.

My cock stiffens as my imagination conjures the image of her hand running over it.

Ignoring my discomfort, I nod. "I traded Bodi some fine lumber from trees that needed to be culled in exchange for this table. You remember Bodi? He was with us when we came to Ov'Ge with Sammi." At her little sound of agreement, I continue. "Few realize it, since he makes a show of being a loud-mouthed warrior, but Bodi is a highly skilled carpenter. It runs in his family and he has quite the passion for it. He can even identify raw wood right down to where it came from just by its scent," I explain with a laugh.

She gives me a disbelieving look but laughs as well.

"And what do *you* enjoy doing, Cavek?"

As we eat, I consider saying something smutty and flirtatious as I normally would, but the earnest expression in her eyes gives me pause. I swallow and decide to show her a part of my life I have never shown anyone, with the exception of my sister, Mimi.

"Well... uh... I enjoy competitive archery contests and hooking yarn."

She blinks slowly. "You mean, like crocheting? Making blankets, and scarves and such."

I shift uncomfortably. If my brothers ever knew this, they would never let me live it down. "Sometimes. Actually, I prefer to make soft toys filled with cotton fibers for the very small children in our territory. One of my sisters distributes them for me at the market."

I am not sure what to expect. Hooking—or crocheting as she calls it—is not typically a craft lauded for males to engage in, especially not a large, strong male such as myself. My reputation is largely because of my marksmanship skill among our people.

Her face softens. "Can I see them?"

I stare at her, unsure of what to do for a long moment. before scrambling up from the table awkwardly. She actually wants to see my work. That wasn't the reaction I was expecting. But I'm not even sure what I was expecting. A sudden eagerness fills me as I go over to a padded seat draped with furs and pull out a large trunk from behind it.

Kate is looking over my shoulder as I pop it open to reveal several soft wool animals and even a few trollbies I had carefully crafted, complete with yarn hair. She lifts one of the trollbies and cuddles it against her chest.

"These are wonderful, Cavek! And you make these for the children? I'm sure they love them. I know these will all find good homes, but we should keep this one for our son."

I nearly burst with pride as I watch her set the small doll aside on the table. She then proceeds to look through all the various dragons, unicorns, mawu, and various beasts found around Ov'Gorg. She leaves not one untouched or unadmired.

"What about you, Kate. What do you like to do?" I ask as she smiles at a small delfass toy with oversized fangs. Kate looks up at me and a small puzzled frown mars her brow.

"I'm not sure anymore. I had so many interests before Boukie was born. I love everything fantasy, going to conventions, gaming, but I've had so little time for myself I don't know what I like to do anymore. Aside from drink coffee and long for a few peaceful minutes with a book or my favorite video game. I really don't know what my passions are. And it's not going to get any clearer with a new baby," she observes with a tired smile.

I trace my finger down her cheek.

"You will discover yourself again, I'm sure," I say softly.

She leans into my touch and my breath stills in my body, my senses clamoring for her, until suddenly the door is flung open and Serus tromps in with Boukie hanging from his neck, squealing with laughter. Cavekji is wide awake and drooling on his finger stuck firmly in his mouth.

"Serus, why is my son trying to eat your finger?" I ask with alarm.

My brother grunts as he swings Boukie and gently deposits her on the chair beside us before peeling my son off his finger. Cavekji immediately starts to howl angrily.

"That is why," my brother grumbles. "Letting him slobber on me was the only way to silence him."

I take my son from him and immediately notice the terrible odor emitting from him as he squalls in a fit of troll-worthy temper. I have to smile with pride because he's clearly a strong little male—but only for a second before the heinous smell assaults my senses. I attempt to hand him off to his mother, but Kate just laughs and steps back. I scowl at her but she holds her hands up with a mischievous smile.

"Oh, no. I don't think so. You want to be a daddy? Now you get to change his ass like a daddy does while I help Boukie get ready for bed. I'll come back and feed him as soon as she's settled for the night."

My jaw drops in dismay when she turns her back on me *and leaves*.

Serus peers down at him, his nose wrinkled.

"So, how are you going to do this?"

I swallow and grimace. My ears are now starting to ring too.

"Hand me the bag that we brought with us with his baby things in it. I saw Kate get his ass-covering from there. I am sure there are more."

My brother heads over to the bag while I slowly peel back the cloth covering. The smell is so wretched my eyes begin to water. How is this even worse than the disposable butt-covering that was in the waste receptacle? A small pack of moist cloths is shoved under my nose just in time. I start to wipe but to my alarm it is sticking terribly. What in the world was this substance made of? Serus clicks with disgust as he watches over my shoulder.

Several cloths later, my son's bottom is clean, and I set the clean butt-covering beneath him ready to close it up around him when his little male part that has been standing up the last several minutes suddenly shoots off, a long arc of pee smacking me in the mouth.

I stumble backward, sputtering in horror. My cursed brother, being no help at all, laughs his ass off. I narrow my eyes at my offspring who has finally ceased crying and is now watching me with what I suspect is a puzzled air.

I take a deep breath and release it, wipe off my face, and smile down at my son.

"That's okay, Cavekji. I know I don't know what I am doing, but we are figuring it out."

Kate giggles from the corner of the room, and like a goddess of blessed she grace sweeps in and nudges me out of the way. With a quick hand, she demonstrates how to fasten his butt-covering before pulling him up into her arms. I nudge my brother to look away as she frees a breast to nurse our son.

Serus excuses himself, leaving us alone in the quiet of our common room. I scoot in beside her, my hand gently exploring my son's round legs and arms and his belly fattened by his mother's milk.

Everything about the moment is a wonder to me, from his small claw-tipped fingers and toes to the beads of milk rolling down his chin as he suckles. He is soundly asleep in what feels like only a few minutes, and his mouth relaxes and releases my mate's reddened nipple. I curve around the two of them, myself drowsy, and cannot imagine a more perfect end to my day.

All those months locked in captivity, I never imagined this.

The light dims outside as night falls and the bioluminescent flowers slowly close their petals when Kate shifts off the seat. I follow her into the bedroom where she tucks Cavekji into the small bed Serus had brought over earlier in the day, before she climbs into our bed.

Ignoring my painfully stiff cock, I strip down to my breeches and crawl in bed beside her, our bodies nestling close together beneath the blanket, providing warm comfort throughout the cool night.

CHAPTER 12

KATE

"And what exactly are you expecting to do with that?"

I stare at the narrow spears in Cavek's hand. Cavekji is drooling on my shoulder as he happily sucks on it. After a few days with the trolls, I've gotten so used to referring to my baby by his troll name that at times I have to struggle to recall how familiar it was to call him CJ.

The time has passed almost too quickly. Lazy days with my family, when Madi is not stealing the children away to give us necessary bonding time, followed by steamy evenings making out with Cavek after the kids are in bed. I can almost imagine that this is the kind of thing I have been missing out on—a normal married life.

Well, as normal as one can get with a troll.

"We're going fishing, remember?" Cavek reminds me with a small frown.

"Yes," I drawl slowly. "But usually that involves poles, lines, and hooks. What am I supposed to do with a spear?"

"Line? Pole?" His brow furrows for a second before it relaxes again. An understanding grin lights up his face and he chuckles. "We don't use such things. This is a fishing spear. You fish with it."

I look at the willowy spear doubtfully.

"I don't know, Cavek. I've heard that hunting fish with a spear is pretty difficult, and I'm not really sure how this activity qualifies as courting either."

Some of the troll courting activities so far have been pretty familiar. We've had quiet dinners with romantic lights. Walks around the lotus pond near the den. We even spent a lovely afternoon at the weekly market. It was filled with beautifully died silks and delicious smelling foods.

Cavek explained that the nearest large market is at the orc village, but it's a two-day journey, so most trolls do small trading among each other here and leave it to merchants to acquire goods from other merchants at the larger market.

The night before was a big full moon celebration. The trolls, considering themselves children of the moon mother, have big dances and feasts during the full moon. While Madi watched the children, we went out, drank our fill of troll-brewed wine, which seemed twice as potent as anything I ever had back home, and danced wildly to the loud drums, horns and lutes of the local musicians.

But spearfishing? It seems... a bit more like work than a date.

Cavek snorts. "It's not too difficult. It will be fun! Serus is taking Boukie today. He says he has a surprise planned for her. He knows how important today is."

I willingly completely bypass this vague "surprise" Serus has planned for Boukie. It can't be too bad. It's a surprise for a seven-year-old, after all. Instead, my mind boggles over the concept of going fishing as an important day for us.

"It's that important?" I ask weakly. Fish guts doesn't sound like romantic bonding. I went fishing a grand total of one time, and never had any desire to repeat the experience. It was boring, the mosquitos bit the hell out of me, and the fish stank. Worst of all, the guy I was with was more interested in fishing and completely ignored me.

Cavek nods as he inspects the edge of one of the spearheads.

"Fishing is one of the important bonding rituals for trolls," he explains. "As you have likely noticed, we subsist largely on different sorts of fish that live in our streams and waterways. Fishing secures dependency between mates, as they must depend on each other and work together." He flashes a grin.

I dredge up an answering smile. I'm still not thrilled about it, but since it sounds very important to him culturally, I'm game to give it a try. A bit of fish guts isn't going to hurt me.

A loud shout draws my attention. I look out the window to see Serus leap easily over a large root, a broad grin on his face. To my surprise, rather than the usual silk or cotton spun weaves, he's wearing a leather tunic and is carrying a child-sized version of the same kind. I frown. What exactly are they doing that requires such sturdy attire?

Cavek sets down his spears and draws up to my side, his lips curving into a small smile moments before Serus throws the door open with a bit more strength than necessary. Cavek winces as the door crashes open but greets his brother with enthusiasm as they pound each other on the shoulder.

"Any word on the activity from the Warue?"

His brother's smile falters and Serus shakes his head grimly. "Nothing concrete. Father is sending me out with my warriors to relieve Garol and his set. They have been reporting increased activity but no recent forays into our territory since we have retrieved you. Lately they have been having altercations with the western Evarue, which is surprising. It is rare for the wolves to encroach on each other's territories. Father wants me to scout it out with my males."

Cavek's brows knit together. "I should be taking this turn and relieving Garol. That is our usual rhythm."

My gut clenches and a whisper of unease flows through me at the idea of Cavek going up against these wolves again. I know he's more than capable but, although he hasn't spoken about much of his time with them, I've seen the brutal scarring that runs from his shoulder to his haunches. What he lived through was nothing short of cruelty, and I can't bear the thought of anything like that happening to him again.

Relief sweeps through me when Serus chuckles. "While you are courting your mate? Father would never get a peaceful night of sleep if he sent you out on rotation. Mother would see to that." He thumps Cavek playfully on the shoulder before looking around the common room and calling out, "Where is my Boukie?"

A small shriek is all that proceeds her as my little ball of terror comes flying into the room from her bedroom.

"Here I am, Uncle Serus!" she says as she sprints across the room and flings herself at him, both arms wrapping around his forearm. Without even breaking a sweat, he lifts her high into the air until she is able to climb up onto his shoulders.

"I brought something for you," he announces proudly as he shakes out the tiny tunic. Boukie makes all the sounds of a child duly impressed.

"May I ask what she's going to be doing that she needs to wear leather for?" I ask suspiciously.

Serus flashes an innocent smile at me. "We are going to see the litter of pups today, and the little guys can get excited. It is just to give a bit of extra padding."

"Oh, you're taking her to visit puppies?" That's not so bad. It just means I am going to end up enduring hours of begging and pleading when she gets back. Maybe it's finally time to find a nice, quiet pet for her.

"Puppies!" Boukie clamors, making the males chuckle at her delight.

"Mother's bitch birthed a litter a couple of months ago. I thought Boukie might like a look before they go to join their new hunting packs."

"And this is going to be safe, right?"

"Perfectly safe," he agrees, baring those sharp teeth at me in a wide smile. I'm never going to get used to trolls' jagged teeth.

"All right then. Be good, Boukie," I remind her, and as a subtle caution for Serus to keep her under control, but Cavek merely winks at her. Not even Boukie at her worst seems to deter the trolls. They find everything she does hilarious. But according to Cavek, trollbies are destructive little things, so trolls naturally have a high tolerance for wild antics. I can only hope that being half-human tempers Cavekji's wild troll half. For my sanity.

"Well, hurry and bring me the trollbie and we will be on our way," Serus laughs as he bounces Boukie on his shoulders. "Mother is beyond thrilled to have him again."

Cavek disappears down the hall and returns with Cavekji. My little sound sleeper must not even have stirred when his father picked him up. He hands his brother the diaper bag, which he immediately shoulders. He's far less forthcoming with his son, however. I watch Cavek's arms tighten around him briefly before reluctantly handing the baby to Serus. It's obvious that he still has trouble letting his son out of his sight. Serus gently cradles him with one arm, his other hand lightly gripping Boukie's leg to keep her balanced.

Cavek is completely still as he watches his brother leave with the children, every muscle tense as anxiety rolls off him in waves. I sidle up behind him, wrap my arms around his waist, and lean into him with my cheek against his back.

"Are you all right? We can always have him bring them back."

His rough hand lands on mine, caressing the bare skin of my forearm. He releases a lengthy sigh.

"No, they will be fine. It will be good for them. Communal raising rears strong young with firm ties to their people and each other. I just worry. I'm afraid after my experiences I expect werewolves to jump out of every shadow," he laughs in obvious self-mockery.

I give his waist a gentle squeeze, conveying my silent support the best way I know how. He runs his hand along my arm again before breaking my grip long enough to turn around and face me. His hands thread through my hair as he looks down at me from beneath heavily lidded eyes that flare with desire as his lips tilt upward.

"You know, we can always skip the fish and just elect to stay home. I'm sure we can find something to do together. An *indoor activity*," I say with a suggestive arch of my eyebrows. After days of self-enforced abstinence, I'm ready to indulge in a bit of temptation.

Cavek chuckles, dropping a kiss on the tip of my nose.

"As much as I would love to explore every inch of whatever indoor activity you have in mind, first, we fish. It's important," he says, his eyes shining with a mixture of affection and laughter.

"Very well. You can't blame a girl for trying," I tease as he bends over, showing that fine ass of his, and picks up a basket and our spears. "Onward to the fish then."

~

I'm not exactly sure what I expected fishing to be. It wasn't standing in thigh-deep chilly water staring thirstily at Cavek, naked except for a kind of loincloth around his hips. I gape like a teenager as every muscle in his abdomen and biceps bunches and bulges with tension as he holds his spear angled above the water.

I almost jump out of the water when a fish as long as my leg swims between us, but then his spear comes down in a swift, brutal arc, striking the large fish and pinning it to the riverbed. Cavek grunts as the fish attempts to wiggle free. His eyes dart up to me, his lips curling.

"Uh, love, you want to give me a hand?"

I blink, startled. "Oh, right. What do I do?"

"Just spear the fish from your side and help me hold him in place while I finish him off."

"Sounds simple enough."

Famous last words. I forgot how water distorts how things appear under its surface. My spear lands so far afield of the fish it is embarrassing. As big as the fish is, it's the marine equivalent of missing the broad side of the barn. My second attempt gets closer but my spear gets stuck between two rocks and I pull so hard that when it finally releases, I end up falling backward.

The cold water rushes over me, momentarily dulling my senses before I come up gasping for air. Cavek gives me a concerned look but I wave him off.

"I'm fine," I mutter in response to his silent question.

His lips thin with worry, but he reluctantly nods as I reposition myself over the viciously struggling fish. I have no doubt that he doesn't *need* my help, but that isn't the point of this little exercise. If he did it himself, it wouldn't serve the purpose of this particular courting task. Being submerged seems to have knocked a bit of clarity into me.

Whether he's strong enough to take it on himself isn't the point. We're supposed to work together.

He grins at me , confident shining through.

"Come on, love. The fish is going to expire of old age before you spear it."

I squint at the damned fish, determined that I won't be beat as I thrust once more. I'm so surprised when the spear lodges in the fish that I nearly lose my footing again. My dignity is salvaged as I catch my balance and beam up at Cavek.

His face fills with pride and he leans forward, ignoring the desperate attempts of the fish as it thrashes. I can feel the strain on my arms and back as it struggles to get free. I watch with interest as he pulls out his dagger and, with a bulge of his bicep, plunges it deep into the base of the fish's head, promptly halting all of its efforts to escape.

I try and lean, unsuccessfully, against my flimsy spear; the thing practically bows under the slightest weight, much to my consternation. Exhausted, my entire body shivers as blood slowly curls through the water. Cavek grins up at me as he fills the basket with water and pulls the fish inside of it. I'm impressed to see that it doesn't leak when he pulls it free from the river.

"Marsh weed," he explains as I stare at the basket. "Many females gather it in mid-summer to make water-tight baskets."

I walk up onto the banks and turn to watch him pack the fish. I stare at the way the muscles in his back and asscheeks flex as he bends to rinse his hands and forearms clean in the river. I instantly forget the chill from the water as my temperature shoots up and warm heat dampens my thighs further.

Cavek slowly stands and turns his head, his nostrils flaring as he scents me. I know it's me he smells by the way his eyes enflame as he looks at me. He ascends the banks. It takes no more than a few steps until he's right in front of me, his arms sweeping me up as he backs me into a thick tree.

Without preamble, he thrusts his hand between our bodies and drags his fingers delicately over the slick folds of my sex as his tongue plunders my mouth in a sweeping kiss. My brain short circuits at this sensual attack. I retain just enough presence of mind to wage my own onslaught against him. My tongue slides against his in an erotic battle as I gyrate my hips in a mating dance as old as time.

When his fingers gently rub at my labia with two digits while his thumb and forefinger pluck at my clit, I jerk my hips with so much force that he chuckles into my mouth. He repeats the motion over and over again until my body thrums and dances on the edge of climax. I shudder and shoot over the edge when he pushes two fingers deep within me, thrusting at a vigorous tempo to ride me through my orgasm. I fall against his chest, crying out with pleasure.

His fingers gently slide out of me, and then seconds later his hands grip my thighs, lifting me high against him, my pussy level with his hard, bare length. He moves away and leans down until my back makes contact with the soft grass. Tiny, bright butterflies suddenly wing up all around us from the butterfly-weed and wildflowers mixed within the long grassy turf.

I wrap my legs around him and eagerly accept him as the pierced head of his wide cock slowly pushes into my channel. He groans into my neck as he enters me, stopping when our pelvises meet. He holds me there against him for several minutes while he pants and regains control of himself, allowing me time to become accustomed once again to his size.

I tighten my legs around him, my feet digging into his ass as I push my hips forward. If he isn't going to hurry up and move, I'm going to get this party started. Cavek groans, growls, and nips my neck, leaving an erotic sting. A completely sensual reprimand.

"I'm in control, love," he grunts. "I will bring you pleasure when I am ready to do so."

"Well, hurry up and get on with the pleasuring," I moan, twisting my hips and squeezing myself around his length to get my point across. I take delight in the way his eyes momentarily seem to cross until he pulls back and slams into me, and I'm pretty certain that mine cross then too. His tongue laves my shoulder and trails up and down my neck as he pounds into me. I lift my hips as his snap forward, desperate to draw him deep within me.

Our tempo builds to a frenzy as we fight for dominance. Our bodies crash together, moans rising up like primal cries into the dim atmosphere around us. My pussy flutters with yet another orgasm as I feel him expand within me, his cock pulsating and the tiny ring pierced through the tip nearly vibrating deep within me.

I cry out as he buries himself deep within me one final time and stays there, his teeth grazing my shoulder, pinning me, as his heat spurts and pours within me. That familiar tingling quality that I thought had been a trick of my imagination before sweeps through me as his hot cum hits the walls of my pussy, sending me into a screaming orgasm.

His body curls around mine and he bellows again, his body releasing another hot spurt. His protective posture both keeps the chill of the air off me. His body is stiff and seemingly aware of everything around us until he finally slips free of my body. He rolls into the grass beside me with a content sigh, his arm drawing me up onto his chest as he strokes a hand through my hair.

I swear I see a pixie hover and giggle before darting away as my eyes drift closed, the warm sun and the heat of his body a dual comfort easing me into brief slumber.

CHAPTER 13

CAVEK

I look down at the basket we carry between us, unable to help smiling the entire way home. Kate casts amused glances at me from time to time, but her eyes sparkle with her own happiness. We are returning home exhausted but sated.

"You do realize that we probably have the most dismal catch in all of recent memory," I say thoughtfully. Most troll pairs will fish zealously through this stage of their courting in an attempt to secure bragging rights, but I don't mind at all.

The courting ritual not only satisfied its purpose, but it also finally gave my mate over to me once again. Touching and tasting my female is far better than any other reward. I will never admit as much, but days of lying in celibacy next to Kate have been torture. But seeing the passion mixed with budding new love in her eyes as she drew me into her has been worth it. Kate is worth everything.

"Fine by me," Kate chuckles. "Being happy with just one fish is a perfectly acceptable trade-off for four orgasms."

I hum in agreement as my cock, despite recently sated, surges with desire at the memory of the feel of her around me. I am looking forward to repeating our joining many times over. Perhaps as soon as we arrive home.

My arousal dies quickly when we step through the trees and I see my brother waiting for us in front of our den. He raises a hand in greeting the moment he spots us, but it's nothing compared with the wide smile on Boukie's mud smeared face.

The mud on her face only matches the layers of mud caking her tiny body from the top of her head down to her feet. Her muddy curls stick out at odd angles with bits of straw and twigs protruding from them. Kate sucks in a breath beside me, but I don't think it's entirely due to Boukie's state of complete filth. No, I have no doubt it is due to the wiggling, and equally muddy mawu pup licking at her with its long-forked tongue.

"Boukie! Drop that thing right now!" Kate yells with such alarm that Serus's eyes widen at her and even I nearly jump.

"But Mommy..." Boukie whines, her lower lip poking out as she clutches the pup even tighter to her chest. Its tiny barbed tail wags with joy as it yips in a tiny squeaking voice.

"But Mommy nothing. Put that monster down right now before it bites you. What were you thinking letting her carry that thing?" she snaps at Serus.

"Kate, it is a mawu pup, not a monster," Serus flounders helplessly, his eyes darting as if seeking a quick escape before landing on me with a silent plea for help.

"A *what*?"

"It's a puppy," Boukie says happily, thrusting the little beast toward her mother with delight. "Uncle Serus took me."

Kate reels back from the wriggling mawu. "I thought you were talking about dogs! No dog I've ever seen is covered with blue scales and has four eyes and six legs!"

I shrug helplessly and retrieve my son from Serus. Cradling

Cavekji against my chest, I cut an annoyed look at my brother. He was supposed to show her the pups, not bring her home covered in mud with the runt of the litter. I don't enjoy the hunt the way many members of my family do. I have no use for a mawu. Even if I did, this one is half the size of a pup its age. It never would have been accepted into a hunt-pack.

"I wanna keep him," Boukie protests, her eyes widening pitifully at us. I almost capitulate then and there but Kate is made of iron and apparently, despite being a warrior for a great many years, I am not.

"Rebecca, I mean it. You can't keep it," Kate says firmly, stepping back from the pup as it swipes its serpentine tongue at her.

I watch in horror as Boukie's face crumbles, big tears rolling down her cheeks as she draws in ragged sobs. I exchange a panicked glance with my brother. I don't have any idea what to do with this. I will happily let her have the pup and anything else just to make her cease her crying.

"But Mommy, all his brother and sisters got homes. He's all alone. He didn't have a family. He needs a family," she finishes on a long wail. The pup twitches it long ears and tilts its head back to howl in accompaniment.

"I hardly think that's the end of the world for him," Kate grits out from between clenched teeth.

Serus widens his eyes earnestly. It's a ridiculous expression on the face of a grown male troll, especially one who is considerably larger than the average male of our species. He brushes a dark lock of dusky purple hair out of his face which somehow makes him all the more endearing to females. It makes me sick. And I do *not* appreciate him trying to manipulate my mate in such a way. I growl a low warning and his eyes flicker with consternation.

My fool of an older sibling pushes on anyway, though with slightly less exaggerated sweetness.

"Truly, Kate, Boukie is right. The pup is the runt of his litter and without a hunt-pack or someone to bond with, it would have eventually grown ill and died. Mawu are not meant to be solitary creatures. Now that he is bonding with Boukie, he will be both a companion and a protector for her."

"He looks dangerous," Kate states bluntly.

"Not to his family he isn't," I grudgingly admit. "There is no better animal than a mawu."

"I'm not sure how comfortable I feel waking up in the same house with what looks like a demon dog coming to me for its breakfast every morning."

The mawu's four electric green eyes fasten on us as it whimpers. I can't say I blame Kate. Unlike delfass kittens, who at least look cuddly, a mawu is as far from cuddly as one can get.

Kate sighs and looks at me at length. "Do you endorse keeping it?"

I shift uneasily, trying not to look at Boukie's pleading eyes.

"I am not particularly prepared to have a mawu in the house, but it wouldn't hurt Boukie to have him. Many families have hunt-packs. You would be hard pressed to find many trollbies without a mawu or two following them around," I admit.

"When I was a trollbie, having a fully grown trained mawu was considered something of a status symbol," Serus added. "Royal children are expected to have them. Although he is a runt, she will probably fit in better with him at her side."

I glare at my brother. He's not helping. To my surprise, Kate makes a small noise that indicates agreement. I never would have expected to be swayed by that sort of argument.

"She does seem awfully attached to him already… If it's that normal for a child to have a mawu, I don't want her to feel singled out by not having one," she mutters, her brow furrowing. "Just how big is he going to get?"

I arch an eyebrow at Serus. He gets to break the news to her. After all, this was his brilliant idea.

My brother coughs. "A full grown mawu is a little larger than a delfass. They are not only working beasts in the hunt but favored mawu serve as mounts." As my mate's eyes widen in horror, he rushes to add, "But Boukie's mawu will be much smaller than that. Still of a size where she can ride him, but he would never carry the larger, heavier frame of a troll."

"So he's a monster," she breathes.

"Just a little one," Serus agrees with a snort.

Crossing her arms over her chest, she looks down at Boukie's hopeful face.

"There will be some ground rules…"

Boukie eagerly nods, a wide smile breaking out over her face.

"He will not terrorize our house…"

"No, Mommy," Boukie agrees.

"You will feed him…"

"Yes, I promise," Boukie says excitedly, holding her pup closer to her.

Kate sighs and for a moment I can imagine how my mother felt when my brothers and I brought baby ciroons home and begged to keep them. The long-eared flying rodents ravaged our mother's gardens for years during their nominally short lifespans. Faced with this now, I think I owe my mother a huge apology. Despite being a runt, the mawu is going to turn our den upside-down until he outgrows his pup phase.

"Okay," Kate finally concedes and shakes her head as Boukie and Serus slap palms together. I am confused by this gesture, but it must have some celebratory meaning among humans that Boukie taught him. I growl as I feel the barest stir of jealousy that my brother is bonding with my daughter more than I am at this moment. I know I must focus on my mate, but I don't want another male stepping in my place with my children either.

With Cavekji tucked in close to me, I crouch down beside Boukie and lean forward, evading the whip-like tongue to scratch the beast behind the ears.

"What will you call him? Vor? Emu? Ora?" I suggest helpfully, drawing on the names of some of the finest mawu males I have heard of.

Boukie frowns and shakes her head.

"No…" she says thoughtfully. "He looks like Stitch to me. I'm gonna call him Stitch."

Kate suddenly giggles. When I raise my eyebrows, she laughs harder.

"Sorry, Cavek," she snickers as she wipes tears from her eyes. "She's naming him after her favorite cartoon alien who's not much bigger than Lucy's chihuahua."

The irony catches me so off guard that I begin to laugh as well. The only one in the dark is Serus, but even he wears a content grin, pleased that everything worked out well.

When Kate finally regains control over herself, she levels a firm glare at Serus and points at him in such dire warning that it makes my brother's smile falter. I feel a bloom of lust rise in me at the ferocity of my female. She is exquisite, and she is all mine.

"Now for you. Since you were generous enough to offload a puppy on me, just keep in mind that someday when you least expect it, I *will* get you back. Come on, Boukie. Let's get you cleaned up."

Boukie sets the pup on the ground and calls, "Come on, Stitch. Let's go inside!"

"Hold it!" Kate shouts, making the child and her pup tumble to halt.

"You and Stitch are going to stand right out here while Cavek and I fetch water to rinse you off. I'm not having you bring an entire mud pit inside."

It is with much laughter and some outraged squealing—especially when due to some slip of the hand Kate is accidentally doused with a bucket of water, which results in an immediate attack on my person with her own supply—that we finally get both pup and child clean enough to go indoors and throw the pair into the bath.

Boukie sits in the tub, blowing bubbles at Stitch who snaps his teeth happily at them from where he sits across from her in the water. Kate and I work together to scrub the pair of them down with soap. Somehow, I got stuck with the mawu, which turned its head to lap at me every half minute. Its tail agitated the water the entire time as I attempted to clean all the folds and scales of the slippery beast, much to Boukie's delight.

The sight of them curled together on her bed, one slender arm wrapped around Stitch, fills me with a strange sort of contentment. Just maybe this is another step to becoming a family. A smelly and generally unpleasant one, but still sweet in its own way.

CHAPTER 14

CAVEK

I wake up in the darkness again. It's all around me. There is nothing but the fetid stench of my cell and the half-rotten bits of food they try to feed me. I scrape off the little that is edible and do my best to sustain myself. I can hear my guard's taunting laughter. Every day passes much like the last. I have no sense of time apart from the one time a week they drag me out of my hole and torture me.

He whispers through the cell bars that he is looking forward to it. He always looks forward to my pain and humiliation.

My body shudders with dread as I hear him come closer and closer.

He whispers promises of what he is going to do to me. I can smell his excitement on him and my stomach heaves, desperate to empty itself of what little nutrition that sustains it.

I shake my head. No, this isn't right. I cannot be here again. I shout out. Where is my son? Where is my mate? The guard laughs. *I have no one here*, he reminds me. *My mate and my son are nothing but a dream*, he says, as he reaches through the bars and drags his claws against my hip. Agony of the like I have never felt rises in my heart and I howl with rage and despair as he laughs at my misery.

I will never escape this place.

∾

Kate

It's the low keening howls that wake me. I turn in the dim golden light and look over at Cavek. He lies curled in on himself on the opposite side of the bed, shivering. His claws tear rivets into the bedding beneath him that will once again need to be mended. In the many weeks I've been here with him now, he seems to have suffered from some unknown night terror. One he refuses to share with me. I feel helpless as I hear him call out wordlessly, broken up only by vicious growls and snarls at his invisible tormentors.

I crane my neck to check on Cavekji. To my relief he's still sound asleep, a pudgy fist curled up against his now apple green cheek. I slide across the mattress, careful to not get too close in case he mistakes me for his attacker.

"Cavek, wake up," I call out to him. "Come on, babe. Come back to me. There's no one here but us. Wake up, my love."

I repeat this refrain over and over until his muscles finally relax and his labored breathing evens out as he's released from his nightmare. He turns toward me, the glow of his purple eyes focusing on me in the weak light of the early morning. He breathes out slowly.

"Kate," he whispers with such love and longing it nearly breaks my heart. He's hoarse from his frantic cries.

"Yes, I'm here," I soothe. I scoot over and wrap my arms around him. He relaxes into my embrace, his entire frame shuddering in relief.

"Thank the gods," he murmurs so low I barely hear him.

I stroke my hand up and down his back.

"Do you want to tell me about it?"

Every time I've asked, he refuses. He stills beneath my touch and goes utterly silent. My heart sinks. He isn't going to share with me

"I do not want to burden you with this. Nor do I wish you to look at me any differently," he says, his words almost tremulous. He draws back to look down at me, his eyes shining. "I want you to see the male I was when we met. That is how I want you to see me. Not broken."

I'm almost numb with shock and then regret sets in. I had no idea he felt that way. That he assumed that I'd ever think less of him for surviving. I stroke a hand down the heavy scars marking his flesh.

I never told him anything about how I really felt for him. He's shown me his love in every action, but I never showed him that I love him. Sure, we've joked a lot, but I have been doing the same old, same old. Shielding my heart.

If there were anyone I could trust with my heart, it's Cavek.

"I love you, Cavek. Nothing you could say would ever make me love you any less. I've seen these scars and they're just another part of you. They weren't there when we met, but that doesn't change the way I feel." I take a deep breath and let it out. "I'm trusting you with my heart. Please trust me with this."

His eyes widen and then star-like tears gather in his lashes, glimmering with some unknown magic as they fall and glide along his face. My breath hitches at the sight.

"I love you too," he rasps around his tears.

"Tell me."

He draws me and tucks me against his chest, my cheek nestled against the hollow of his neck. I can feel the thudding of his heart and I turn my head to press my lips against it.

"When the werewolves captured me, for the first week they tortured me endlessly. All to discover the hidden entrance in the magic protecting our kingdom. You see, Kate, no one can enter our kingdom without either a troll to show them or knowledge of the secret entrance. I refused, so they did everything they could think of to degrade, hurt, and shame me. My guard took particular pleasure in it.

"When they couldn't break me, they threw me in a dank cell with every intention of letting me rot there. Once a week, they would pull me out to torture me again. Every week my guard would laugh as they prepared to haul me out, and I could smell his excitement. When I dream, sometimes they're good dreams, but sometimes they take me back to those moments and I am alone in my misery without you and our family," he says as his body trembles with lingering distress.

I stroke his hair, feeling the urge to cry for him but I blink back my tears, trying to stay strong for his sake. My mate survived through months of terrible abuse.

"I'm so proud to have such a strong male who wants me of all females for his mate," I whisper around the emotion thick in my throat. "What can I do, Cavek?"

His arms tighten around me. "I just want to forget. I want only your touch and scent with me."

I draw up and meet him halfway, our lips sliding against each other. The kiss is a sweet give-and-take as our tongues dance with each other. I feel Cavek's desperate embrace as our kiss changes from sweet to frantic, a brutal reflection of his need for connection.

I meet his need with my own when I realize that I could have

THE TROLL BRIDE

actually lost him—lost all of this—during those terrible months that he suffered. The desire to connect and affirm our bond is a living, breathing thing that rages within me.

I need all of him. All his pain and happiness.

I shiver as I feel the sting of his sharp teeth grazing my bottom lip as he sucks it in between his own and tugs on it. His claws erotically dig ever so slightly into the flesh of my ass as he pulls me tight against him.

With a shaky gasp, I pull away and sink back down into the bedding and chuckle as Cavek's arm tightens around me.

"Going somewhere, love?" he growls with his desire-roughened voice.

My pussy drips sopping wet with the heat of my arousal.

"Is there somewhere you'd like me to go?" I murmur as I slide my fingers down his taut emerald abs until they come to rest and curl around his thick shaft. That part of him leaps eagerly against my palm, the tip of dewing with a pearl of precum that I rub over the head of his cock.

I pump his length a few times in my hand, and Cavek turns his head and groans into his pillow. His arms release me so that his claws can dig into the mattress. The only thing at risk is the condition of our bedding as I begin my southward journey.

"Gods be merciful," he gasps as my tongue sweeps over the tip a few times before I suck him into my mouth.

My tongue toys with his piercing as I suck and stroke his cock with my tongue. I take it as deep as my unfortunately superior gag reflex allows. But I make it good for him. I pump the base that doesn't fit in my mouth with one hand, and with the other I stroke and fondle his balls, making him shudder with his rapidly rising pleasure.

His fingers tangle in my hair and a tremor rips through me. I expect him to take control of the pace, but I'm surprised when he pulls me off his cock and flips me onto my belly. His hands draw my hips up and my pussy pulsates with a fresh flow of heat and desire. Cavek growls and he blankets me with his body, his cock nudging against my entrance.

I'm surprised that I feel no impulse to fight against his obvious dominance. Instead, everything within me submits in this moment. I lower my head and pant into the bedding as he brushes his cock against my clit, teasing the entrance of my sex with slow deliberate pumps of his hips. He licks at my shoulder, running his tongue back and forth in small circles.

"Mine," he rumbles. "My mate."

"Yes," I moan. "Forever."

His cock twitches against me and he chuckles.

"Forever. I will never let you go now. I'm sealing you to me," he growls seconds before clamping his teeth onto my shoulder. I shriek but the sudden burst of pain flees under a flood of intense pleasure. What is that? I can feel something pump slowly into my veins, leaving a hot, erotic burn as it fills me.

A hum runs through my body, drawing a sharp orgasm at the same moment his cock dives into me. My ass shakes with each rough thrust, my arms and shoulders trembling from the exertion of keeping myself braced as he rocks into me. His sack slaps rhythmically against my clit every time he drives forward. One orgasm spirals into another and I pant, moan, and writhe, my voice joining with his deep grunts and growls.

My body tightens as he swells inside of me as he drives deep within and grinds against me. The release of his hot seed triggers my own climax, my scream rising with his roar. Together we collapse onto the bed, a mass of sweaty limbs and sweet drawn-out kisses as we pet each other. He spends several minutes licking his bite mark. I feel a fizzling burn all along the punctured skin and the area he marked from my neck to my shoulder. After several minutes he pulls back and settles against me.

"We did that a bit out of order," he says with a wry note to his voice.

"How so?" I ask, snuggling into him.

"Traditionally, I'm not supposed to do that until our mating ceremony. I would mark you publicly."

"Mark me?"

I feel him nod. "Our bites heal quickly but I secrete a special saliva during mating that not only heals the bite but stains the skin around it."

A giggle burst out of me. "Honestly, as stimulating as it was, I think that would be a bit embarrassing if we did it in front of anyone else."

I feel his body behind me shake with his deep laughter.

"Naturally, we're still going to have the ceremony. Mother will insist. We aren't the first pair to succumb to the need to seal themselves to one another before the formalities are taken care of."

I grin as he nuzzles my neck, kissing the delicate skin there again. I could stay in his arms forever.

A small whimper from Cavekji's basket draws us out of our contented worship of each other. Cavek leans his forehead against my own.

"I think our son may need to be moved to his own room soon," he laughs and kisses me soundly before sliding off the bed.

I admire the flex of his ass as he walks over to the basket and bends over. The horrible scarring from shoulder to thigh doesn't detract at all from the beauty of his muscles in motion. I smile as he stands back up, cradling our son to his chest. He's whispering something to our son, a blissful expression on his face as he brings Cavekji back to bed with us.

Nestled between our bodies, our son yawns, his brilliant eyes slowly blinking as he falls back to sleep. As I lie there, I'm not really watching him; I'm watching my mate. His pale lavender hair falls over his face like a gossamer curtain and his black lips tilt up as he smiles down at Cavekji. His glowing eyes flick back up to me and he settles deeper into the bed, his thick arm wrapping around both of us in a protective embrace.

CHAPTER 15

CAVEK

With our mate bond sealed and the courtship period concluded, our lives as a family slip into an easy pace. To my surprise, we hadn't even needed to tell Boukie. The moment we left our room the next morning, Boukie came running out of her room with Stitch tumbling after her and declared that I'm her daddy now. She didn't give me much time to dwell on it before she was up in my lap. I may not have sired her but, in that moment, I knew she was mine. My daughter. Life transitioned to the quiet pace of family life, and I found that I treasured each of those days even more.

Not that I don't have my responsibilities. Now that Kate and I are no longer courting, and word of that didn't take long to reach my parents, I have resumed most of my previous duties, including alternating patrols around our territory. Despite being taken away for hours on end, having a family to come home to makes it all worthwhile. Kate and our children—even with the mischief Boukie gets up to with Stitch—make my life one of peace and contentment when I'm not having to bash thick-skulled heads together when some of the males around here get out of control.

I'm still concerned about the Warue, but even Serus, upon returning from the northern border, has assured me that the tribe isn't showing any interest in the border or attempting to slip over into our territory. It's like they are ignoring our very existence. Rather than celebrate, my brothers and I agree that the whole thing is highly suspicious. Yet it has had its indirect benefits.

To my surprise, the regular conflicts between the tribes bordering our territory have had one truly positive impact on our kingdom. The Evarue on our western border have broken their silent isolation from the world and have opened up peace talks between our peoples. Representatives from the tribe are coming today to meet with us, and Mother and Father have specifically asked me to be present, as one of the most diplomatic members of our family.

I am digging through the trunk looking for one of my better silk tunics when I hear the front door slam. Kate had gone out just minutes before to look for Boukie to get her ready to attend with me. By that sound, it seems she isn't too happy.

Plucking up the deep blue silk tunic I make my way into the common room and come to a grinding halt. The stench nearly does me in, attacking my sensitive nose, but the sight before me stops me where I stand. I try to hold my breath and venture closer, but it doesn't help. My daughter watches me with a sheepish smile.

"Hi, Daddy," she squeaks.

I frown down at her, showing my displeasure while I try to ignore the sentimental assault. It's not an easy task, especially when her eyes widen as they fill with unshed tears and her lower lip juts out with a quiver. Thankfully, the smell coming off her is so nauseating that it keeps my mind focused on what is important.

I wrinkle my nose and try to breathe only through my mouth.

Boukie is standing on a chair, where Kate doubtlessly set her, covered in a reeking mixture of prized fertilizer, mud, and chicken feathers. A *lot* of chicken feathers. Even Stitch, sitting at the foot of the chair, has feathers and muck caught in his scales.

Kate returns to the room with a bucket of soapy water, her nose wrinkled with a distaste I would expect from any reasonable being that possesses a nose.

"Boukie, how the hell did you end up in the neighbor's coop?" she asks as she dunks a heavy sponge into the water.

"Mommy, that's a copper for the swear jar," she says around a trembling sob. I almost admire her tenacity in the face of punishment. Yet part of me is amused because the swear jar has become the bane of me and my brothers. She may be small and human, but she possesses the ears of a night-flier.

My mate isn't as easy to sway. She scowls fiercely at our daughter as she strips the soiled garments off her and hands them to me. I don't want them but accept them anyway. I pinch them between my thumb and forefinger and, opening the door, I fling them out into the garden. Might just be best to burn them. I don't know if I want to touch them again. Once was enough. I don't know how Kate can stomach cleaning Cavekji's filth. My mate is a brave, strong female.

When I return, Boukie has been wiped clean and is wearing a fresh tunic.

"Mommy, I didn't mean to do it! Stitch saw the chickens and was chasing them. I was just trying to get him to stop. But when I was carrying him out, I tripped and fell in the yuck," she says pitifully.

Kate snorts with irritation. I stifle a chuckle, but I can't keep my lips from twitching. I imagine that Bishol had a good laugh over it.

"I hope you at least apologized to Bishol," Kate says wearily as she attempts to wipe down stitch and Boukie nods with earnest solemnity. The graveness with which they are treating the moment is too much and I begin to laugh, making my sweet mate scowl at me.

I duck the sponge she throws at me and hold my hands up. "I'm not laughing at you, mate, but you worry too much. Trolls have a different perspective on such mischief. No doubt Boukie gave him quite a bit of entertainment. In fact, it is the rest of us you should feel sorry for, because no doubt it will be his favorite story to tell everyone of how the little princess fell in his fertilizer pile next to the chicken coop."

I watch a small smile reluctantly tug at Kate's lips as I pull on my tunic. It's almost a shame. I know that my mate loves to gaze upon my bare torso. Unfortunately, while my mother would find it splendidly romantic, my father would not be as impressed if I didn't at least try to be presentable for our visitors.

While Kate retreats to our chamber to change, I go into Cavekji's new room. My son is awake and babbling to himself. I smile down at him and watch him play with his feet. He has become interested in grabbing and exploring everything within reach lately. The minute he sees me, a wide, toothless smile stretches over his face. Making silly noises at him, I reach over the tightly woven walls of his well-padded bed, lift my son into my arms, and proceed to ready him.

Waiting in the common room for us, Kate is a glorious sight in her saffron yellow dress, her dark hair rippling in loose waves down her shoulders. She flashes a nervous smile and I can understand why.

Other than our courting activities, this is our first time socializing in public. There will be members of the troll court she has yet to meet plus meeting the Evarue representatives. It's natural for her to feel nervous. I grew up in that world and even I want to hurl—to borrow a quaint human euphemism—whenever I have to attend a royal function at the palace.

All at once, I want to keep her concealed safely in our den. I don't want her around the werewolves at all. I look down at the slick stain on her shoulder and admire the rainbow play of light over it. At least my mark should deter other males.

~

Kate

I know Cavek tried to warn me before, but I don't know if I really believed him until now. The werewolves are massive creatures and look almost exactly like bipedal wolves, with a short fuzz of fur over hard abs, large humanoid hands, and massive muscled chests and biceps that most human men would kill for. The long hair trailing from the crown of their heads flows loose except for a few braids framing their faces. The rest seems to blend in with the fur coats along their backs. It's almost artistic, the way it fringes the back of their arms and haunches. They're awe-inspiring, intensely masculine creatures.

Madi rushes to greet us, clad in her signature bubblegum pink but accented for the occasion with pink crystals.

"Kate, you're here! I am so happy to hear news of your mating. I told Virol that it would happen so, and here we are. Though I had hoped to have the mating ceremony *before* the mating, who am I to judge? Sometimes, a finely built male is just too hard to resist," she states with a knowing smile.

"I told you, Nana Madi," Boukie giggles. "I told you Cavek's gonna be my daddy very soon."

"Yes, you did, my little trollbie girl," Madi gushes with delight. "And you can help with the mating ceremony. Wouldn't that be nice?"

"Can it be pink?" Boukie squeals, completely on board with the plan.

"But of course! Whoever heard of anything romantic not being pink? I am even having a nice tunic for your new father made in a suitably masculine rose," she says, casting my mate a pleased smile. Cavek tries to swallow back his groan, but he isn't fast enough to keep me from hearing it. I cough over my laugh and smile at my mother-in-law.

Another rough cough alerts us to the presence of one of the werewolves accompanying Garol. Serus mumbles something to Cavek before introducing the large male. And truly, this werewolf is the largest of them. Completely covered with scars, he's a solid black male with amber eyes.

"Cavek... Mother, allow me to introduce you to Eral, Enforcer of the Evarue Tribe. Eral, you of course have heard of our mother, Madi, the queen of the trolls. This is my brother, Cavek, and his mate and children," Garol concludes as his eyes slide over me and my children with quiet dismissal.

He doesn't even bother naming us. We're just extra baggage to him. It's not that Garol doesn't like us; he doesn't find us important enough to even notice. But Cavek assures me that he barely views Cavek worthy of his attention unless he's acting as a liaison. That makes me feel a little better, but I still think he's a complete dick.

Eral proves to be far more charming, even if his focus is a bit unnerving. He inclines his head and smiles. Although he includes Cavek in his greeting, his eyes fasten on me with curiosity.

"A pleasure to meet you all. This is an unexpected treat. Unlike many of my brethren, my duties keep me in Ov'Gorg and I have never had the pleasure of meeting a human. I have heard you are much like we are in breeding form, but far fairer in countenance. I am delighted to see that this was not an exaggeration."

I can feel Cavek bristling next to me. Although Eral hasn't

said anything out of line, his admiration is evident, and my mate takes exception to it.

"Eral, do not tease Cavek," Madi admonishes him. "They are newly mated, and he is going to be territorial for quite a few years before he mellows," she giggles.

The wolf nods to Cavek, a small smile curving the flexible lips of his muzzle.

"My apologies. I did not intend anything untoward in my observation. Simply... admiration," he rumbles, his eyes gleaming.

Madi nudges my mate until he utters a short acceptance, but his arms wrap around me and Cavekji and he positions Boukie behind him as he frowns fiercely. Regardless of his verbal communication, Cavek's territorial stance is loud and clear. Eral is completely unfazed. The atmosphere around us becomes tense as the males size each other up.

"Eral, since we will be allies, you *must* come to the mating ceremony. Bring a few friends. They have already done the deed, sadly, but that has never stopped a troll," Madi says, breaking the silent tension of the moment.

Long canid teeth flash in a wide smile as he accepts the invitation. He turns to signal and two large males, one dark silver and the other purest white, materialize beside him so suddenly that I nestle into Cavek's side.

"Allow me to introduce my brothers. Falo, the beta wolf of our tribe, and Arawl, the tribe guardian."

The queen looks at the them, her face a shrewd mask despite all the pomp of ridiculous color on her.

"Tell me, what is it exactly that the Troll Middling Way Kingdom can do for you?"

Falo doesn't even glance at me. He bares his fangs in a stark smile at Cavek and Madi and for once I'm grateful to be ignored. Where Eral, although a bit much, is charming, Falo is not only rude but almost frightening with the aggressive authority that pours off him. He's not the alpha, but he wears power. That much is evident.

The other brother, Arawl, is the least threatening of the bunch, which makes me suspect he's the younger of the males. He smiles and waggles his claws at Boukie but otherwise looks like he would rather be miles away from here. I can't help but agree.

"We merely wish for aid against a common enemy. The Warue Tribe has attacked both of us. They would have more direct access to our territories if they conquer yours, so it is in our best interest to help you. I am sure you are intelligent enough to see that the Evarue would be advantageous allies for your kingdom," he says with a smirk.

"Perhaps," Cavek says.

He seems reticent in dealing with them and I can't help but to think that he would be able to do his job more effectively if he wasn't trying to guard us from the very males he is trying to negotiate with. I clear my throat and unintentionally draw everyone's attention to me. I blush and lean in to whisper to Cavek.

"I'm going to take Boukie out to the gardens. As we arrived, I saw other children playing out there under the watch of the guard. I think it'd be more appropriate for her than listening to this conversation."

I watch him war with his own thoughts. But at last, he nods his head.

"Don't go beyond the guarded fore-garden," he whispers. I nod as he returns his attention to the werewolves. The white male, Arawl, gives me a sympathetic smile tinged with a bit of longing. Poor guy wants to escape too.

The peace of the gardens is a welcome respite, and I turn Boukie loose to run. A trollbie with fuzzy hair who she seems to know waves at her as she runs to join him. I wander around the flower beds, keeping Boukie in my sight as I admire the flowers.

Between the blooms and keeping watch on Boukie, I'm so distracted that I almost stumble into a small group of female trolls before I hear them.

All of them are clad in the finest pixie-spun silks, with their manes of hair in various shades of lavender and dark purple flowing around their heads and down their backs. More than one has wires laden with gems or flowers knotted into her thick unruly mass of hair. Each of them varies in hue from moss green and jade to the most vivid emerald, almost as bright as that of Cavek. They are tittering and laughing together.

I smile, thinking maybe it would be fun to sit and have someone to laugh with. I haven't had that since Sammi returned to live among the orcs, and I'm hardly shy at making new friends. I straighten my dress and prepare to step out from behind the flowering bushes and join them.

"Can you imagine, Cavek mating a human?" one of them trills with a sharp laugh. I recoil in surprise at the venom in her voice.

"I know. I feel rather sorry for him. There are many beautiful female trolls who would be quite pleased to mate bond with a strong, handsome prince like him despite his ordeal. Yet he would choose a human. Why? They are so… ugly," another giggles.

"Quite plain. You saw her standing there with him, dressed as if she is one of us, but pale and colorless except for that dreary, dark hair. I wonder if she is as dull of wit as she is of color…? What Cavek must go through."

"Please, don't feel sympathy for him. If he wants to mate a beast, let him. She will never be one of us. Others may call her and the ugly child of hers a princess, but *we* are true noble females. She is nothing." The last laughs scornfully.

My heart plummets and I withdraw before they notice my presence. All the trolls I've met have been so welcoming. I try to ignore it, to push the memory out of my mind, until much later in the evening when Cavek proudly introduces me to his two sisters,

Mimi and Vandra. Mimi receives me with all the kindness in the world, but when Vandra nods to me and coolly greets me with a cold flare in her eyes I recognize her voice. She was the last who spoke among the females in the garden.

My eyes dart over to Cavek as he smiles down at his sisters, and I know I can't tell him that she will never accept me.

CHAPTER 16

CAVEK

I stand beside my father as the Evarue males depart for their overnight lodgings. They were offered rooms in the palace, but they had declined on the excuse of finding such surroundings unrestful. I consider that a fair objection, but my whole attention is not on them.

Instead, I'm focused on the fore-gardens where my mate sits alone watching Boukie play with a young male troll. I recognize the male. He is one of the children of a female who coordinates the palace staff. Boukie must have found a friend in him on one of her numerous trips with Serus to visit Mother. It disturbs me that many of the children of the affluential families are giving Boukie a wide berth, but even more so that none of the females of court are even making an effort to be cordial to my mate.

I growl low in my throat and look around helplessly for my sister. Vandra knows all the females and organizes parties and events with them. I believe they are working on the summer solstice festivities. I know that Kate would enjoy that. Her eyes had positively lit up when I told her of our festivals throughout the year.

"Cavek, are you listening to me?" Father says with an impatient sigh.

I turn and meet the stern gaze of my sire. I had known it was a matter of time before Father would have another assignment to take me far away from my family. It's not unreasonable, as my brothers have tasks that also take them away many days at a time, but I don't hate it any less.

"Yes, I hear you."

He nods, pleased. "I know that your mother wishes to organize a mating ceremony for you, but that can wait. Now that you are mated, you are able to fulfill all of your regular duties. The males of the Evarue Tribe are leaving the Middling Way and I wish you to accompany them. Speak to their alpha, observe the activity of the werewolves in general, and report back to me in four days' time."

"If this is a diplomatic mission, perhaps it would be better if I take my family with me, to put the tribe at ease."

"Don't be absurd, Cavek. Females and younglings do not belong on sensitive missions such as this," he scoffs with a shake of his head. "Your family will not expire without you." He clasps a huge hand on my shoulder and squeezes it with all the paternal warmth he can offer. "You will be home with them within just a short time. I know it is difficult when you are newly mated, but this is for the best. You will see."

Kate is not pleased when I tell her as we ready ourselves for bed. Boukie and Stitch are soundly sleeping in the mound of pillows on Boukie's mattress, and even Cavekji fell asleep just as we were arriving home. I hate the look in my mate's eyes when I explain my mission.

I rub my hands along her shoulders. "I won't be gone long. I swear it."

"The last time you went away dealing with werewolves you were lost to me for a year. I don't know if I can bear that again," she whispers in a choked voice.

I nudge my broad nose against her narrow one until she tilts her head up to look at me.

"Don't be silly. That was a completely different tribe. They have another whole syllable to their name. Surely that counts for something," I attempt to poorly jest. Her answering smile is strained but she makes a valiant effort for my sake.

I slip out of our bed in the very early morning. I don't wish to wake my family. I would rather them sleep than watch tearfully as I leave. I don't think my heart can take that. So, silently, I pull on my armor and weapons and grab my bow. It has been so many weeks since I've readied myself for battle it feels foreign. I kiss my mate and Boukie before lingering in the doorway of Cavekji's room. He stirs only briefly, his eyes flickering open before settling back down into sleep.

I pick up his tiny trollbie doll, ready to tuck it back under his arm, but something makes me pause. I raise it to my nose and smell the lingering scents of my family all over it. The touches of Boukie and Kate from when they played with Cavekji, and the stronger scent of my son. Without further thought, I slip it into my pack. I'll be sure to bring it home.

With that final vow, I leave my den and step out into the thick mist.

∼

Kate

I sit at the low table with a basket of tubers, idly peeling the skin off them one by one. Serus sits across from me, a look of concern on his face. It's sweet for him to worry about me, but nothing seems to convince him that it is not necessary.

He holds Boukie in his arms as Cavekji plays on the small rug beside us. I've looked everywhere for his favorite trollbie toy, but I haven't been able to find it, so in a last-ditch effort I pulled a strange animal from the newest collection of beasts that Cavek has been hard at work on.

Just looking at them made me misty-eyed, thinking of Cavek sitting in front of the fire with me in the late hours of the evening, his hands crocheting with practiced ease. Having him gone the last couple of nights has been rougher than I anticipated. The children are handling it well, though. Boukie is confident that her daddy is safe and will be home soon, and Cavekji is blissfully unaware as he chews on the ear of his new toy. Stitch rests just a foot away from him, his bat-like ears sticking straight up, as if just waiting for an opportunity to steal the toy.

Serus sighs. "I do not like leaving you here alone," he complains as he leans over to pick up Cavekji. The baby burbles happily at his uncle as the male sets him on his large knee and begins to bounce him.

"Uh, Serus. I wouldn't bounce him so much. He just ate and he might—"

Too late. My son, in one of his more glorious moments, spits up all over his uncle's lap. Now that he's starting to eat mashed berries and grain, it's colored a bright purplish-pink. Serus looks so horrified that I wince in sympathy but don't bother to hide my chuckle as I pluck him from his uncle's lap so Serus can clean up. I use a spare rag beside me to quickly wipe my son's face.

"Really, Serus. I have a lot I plan on getting done around here today. I can't possibly get away. Truthfully, I'd rather just stay here when Cavek isn't here. But I want you two to go. You know how much Boukie loves visiting Madi at the palace. I insist."

I don't want to tell him that with Cavek with me, I would feel alone in the palace surrounded by the courtly females who pass their days in the palace. Although Mimi was delightful when we met, I dread running into Vandra and any of her ilk any time soon.

Still, Serus doesn't look convinced, and I know why. Rumor has been spreading that Boukie has foresight. Her disturbing accuracy on many things over the last year since humanity was once again contacted by the fae leaves little doubt that it's true.

"Mommy, come with us," Boukie says, her lower lip trembling.

I learn across the table and take her hand, squeezing it gently.

"All right. Let me get a few things done around here while Cavekji naps, and Uncle Serus can come back in a couple of hours and get me. Does that suit everyone?"

Neither look happy but they reluctantly agree and, before long, leave for the palace. I hold Cavekji on my hip as I watch them disappear from sight. My son is fussy today and as soon as they leave, he wails inconsolably. It takes some effort to soothe him into a fitful slumber and I wonder if he's already starting to cut teeth. Trolls develop faster than human babies, but it didn't seem too early for a human baby to begin teething.

I stretch the kink out of my back from a solid hour of stitching and hear a *thump* at the door. I frown impatiently. It's too early for Serus to be back already. I told him to give me a few hours, but it hasn't been more than half that yet.

Excitement stirs within me. Maybe it's Cavek? What if he's back early? And good timing too that we can take advantage of while our son naps.

With a tug, I pull on the door, but no sooner does it open than a sweet strangely familiar scent fills my lungs and I succumb to the darkness of sleep.

I wake what has to be hours later in unfamiliar surroundings. It's cold and dark, with only the faintest light streaming down through the canopy. To my relief, Cavekji sleeps on the moss beside me. A gargantuan mawu stands a few feet away as his rider looks down at me in silence. I cough to clear the lingering effects of the sleep from my chest before speaking.

"What's going on?" I can't keep the fear knotting in my stomach out of my tone.

The rider tilts their head and then slowly a gloved hand comes up and pushes back its hood. I draw in a sharp breath as I see the face of Vandra. Her lips curve into a disdainful smile.

"You recognize me, I see," she says, her voice a soft and throaty purr. "I suppose it is just for you to know who has orchestrated your end. If you had only stayed in Ov'Ge, this never would have been necessary. You were never supposed to come here. I arranged for the Warue Tribe to take Cavek."

She scowls. "They were only supposed to keep him imprisoned for a short time so that he would forget his infatuation with you. I even took measures to ensure that word of your brat would never reach my family. You and that... *thing* are ruining everything! The elves will never allow us to join them in their courts if we mingle our blood with humans," she sneers.

"What are you going to do?" I ask, drawing Cavekji into my arms. He begins to stir as the sleep starts to fade from him.

Vandra touches a hand to her chest innocently.

"Me? I am not going to do anything. I am just leaving you and your brat here in the northern territory, in Warue land. They do so love to tear apart human flesh from what I recall. You thought the Evarue at court were frightening? They are pups compared to the Warue," she laughs cruelly as she pulls her hood back down.

"Goodbye, Kate," she says calmly. With a sharp nudge of her knee, the mawu turns and lopes away, leaving me and my son alone.

I tuck Cavekji against my breast as Cavekji begins to whimper. The few luminous flowers barely produce enough light to see a three-foot radius of the perimeter around me. I shiver as an icy wind sweeps over me, but it's less for the cold and more for the dread in my belly as I hear a savage howl travel on the breeze.

The wolf when he approaches is large but doesn't look as healthy as those I saw at court. His fur is mangy and has many bare spots from years of fights, and his eyes appear to leak a nasty mucus.

There's something very wrong with him.

Cavekji begins to wail as the male stares down at me, menace burning in his features. My heart beats in terror and my eyes widen as he looms closer, his nostrils expanding to scent the air around me. The happy growling sounds as he discovers something that he likes make me shudder.

A large hand with wicked claws snatches me up, hauling me into the darkness.

CHAPTER 17

CAVEK

In the Evarue territory, a break in the trees gives way to a small grassy meadow where several streams feed into a giant lake. The Evarue do not den there, preferring the thick root system to make their home, much like trolls do, but the meadow attracts various animals that they hunt. One particular area closest to the dens has a rocky outcropping where a few of the females and younger males often take the tribe's kits to exercise and play, and where the community itself often converges. Here is where I spend most of my days while with the Evarue Tribe when not in the small den reserved for visitors at the fringe of their community.

The first several days were a difficult adjustment. The nightmare that hadn't plagued me since sealing my mating bond returned with a vengeance, surrounded as I am now deep in werewolf territory. Although I spoke confidently to my mate, it's difficult to remember at times that these are not the same werewolves who held and tortured me. I still sometimes tense when many males are too close to me, much to my shame. I know they can smell the trepidation on me, and I'm thankful when they shift away from me despite my embarrassment. Perhaps they sympathize with me in a fashion, preferring their solitude away from other species.

The werewolves in general are distrustful of outsiders, although curious. Especially the kits. Despite the large size of the males, the females are smaller, only a little smaller than an average-sized female troll. The kits, however, are smaller than trollbies, but this makes sense given that they're born in litters. They are the most inquisitive, following anything that their tiny flicking ears hear, or pinkish noses catch scent of.

I sit cross-legged on a large boulder and watch the kits playing under the patient supervision of the adults lying in the grass or on similar rocks to the one I am perched on. Not for the first time since I've accompanied the Evarue ambassadors into their territory, I miss my family. I look down and am surprised to see that at some point I had pulled out Cavekji's small doll and am clutching it in my hand. I lift it to my nose and draw the slowly fading scents of my family.

"A memento from home?"

I look up as Eral crouches by the boulder. He nods to the small toy in my hands. I allow my fingers to relax and caress the fibers.

"It belongs to my son. It carries the scents of my family. I was driven to take it with me when I left."

Eral tilts his head and looks at it with renewed interest. He delicately sniffs and I clutch the doll tighter, letting loose a low warning growl. He has no business scenting my family. They're mine. The male doesn't respond other than to flick his ears with curiosity.

"I mean no offense," he says stoically. "I was merely curious if the scent was strong enough to give comfort. I understand that with a new mate and such a young offspring, being apart from them must be difficult. Their scents are well-imbued on the doll. It must help. That is a clever way of managing it. Perhaps I will recommend my hunters do the same when we must be apart from our loved ones."

Eral opens his mouth to say something more but a howl goes out and is quickly carried by the other wolves. The male frowns.

"Baru is warning the pack that there is an intruder. A troll." He listens a moment longer before easing back up to his feet. "Falo recognizes him. Your brother approaches."

I grunt in acknowledgment and swing my feet down from the rock just as Serus comes into view. Several werewolves trail close behind him, hackles raised. My brother, in his typical careless manner, seems entirely unconcerned with the threat. Strangely, despite his lack of self-preservation that would demand he at least notice the werewolves reacting with hostility to his uninvited intrusion, he seems anxious.

Something is wrong.

He raises a large hand in greeting and hastens his pace. I stride forward out of concern, meeting him halfway.

My brother's hands immediately come up to grip me with such steely strength it's as if he is holding me in place. His instinctual need to restrain me doesn't bode well. Alarm flashes through me.

"Serus, what—?"

"Cavek," he rasps, emotion stopping his words. "Kate and Cavekji—Cavek, they are gone."

The world drops away from me and I cannot breathe. I feel lost, fumbling in an inner darkness. Kate, my light, is gone? I don't even notice that I dropped the small doll until my brother presses it back into my hands, his eyes brimming with sympathy.

"No, that's not possible."

My brother's grip intensifies, and I don't realize until that moment that I'm struggling against his hold.

"They are gone, Cavek. Whoever is behind it also tried to get Boukie from the palace garden. If it weren't for Stitch—anyway, she is safe," he says soothingly, although I'm not sure if that last part was more for me or for himself.

"What happened?" I manage to pull myself together enough to ask.

My brother grimaces, his eyes dim. "We don't really know. Boukie was playing in the gardens with that young male she befriended. Stitch was raising such a terrible clamor that I, Garol, and several guards rushed out. Stitch's muzzle was covered in blood, so it is obvious he managed to bite whoever tried to take her... but by the gods, it was a near thing."

"Garol went running out?" I mutter in disbelief.

Serus shrugs and he gives me a wan smile. "Garol has some strange priorities, but he is not heartless. And of late, Boukie is the only one who manages to be unoffended by our brother's sour attitude. When Stitch began to bark, I swear to you that he ran faster than any of us to get there."

His smile fell. "Boukie had been crying all day about something not being scary, and a bad person, but none of us knew what to make of it. Boukie couldn't even tell us anything about the attacker other than that it was a bad person all covered up. My guess is that they covered themselves with a hooded cape. She is unharmed, but her friend Bafulk was hit hard enough to leave a sizeable lump on his head when he came to. After Boukie's attack, I went immediately to your den. I am so sorry, Cavek. We have males looking all over the territory for them."

I swallow thickly and nod. It doesn't feel real. Nothing feels real at this moment. Is this another night terror? I don't think so. I don't think even my imagination would have conjured my brother looking so distraught. He didn't even look that way even when they rescued me from the Warue.

I turn to address my hosts.

"My apologies. I must go now."

Eral nods as if he expects nothing else. He lets out a series of low yips and three other wolves slide up beside him, two silvery males and a tawny-colored female.

"With your permission, Alpha Baru, we will assist the trolls. Our kind has a greater ability for tracking once we have their scents. We can do no less for those we wish for our allies."

Baru frowns but reluctantly nods. Falo, however, immediately objects.

"Brother, why should we send any of ours after a human? They are weak and will breed their weakness into the peoples of Ov'Ge. It is likely already dead, and the offspring with it. There is no reason to expend any of our hunters for this. I am certain they would rather remain in our own territories."

Eral bristles and growls. "You do not speak for all of us, Falo."

Distantly, I am aware that the conversation takes an ugly turn, but my mind is elsewhere. There is only the all-consuming need to find my mate and son.

"You all figure it out, but I am going home. If you wish to help us, it is welcome, but do not worry, I will not ask the time of anyone who would consider my mate and son as lesser beings," I snarl, the last aimed directly at Falo.

The male flattens his ears, his fur bristling, but Baru quells him with a single glance.

"Although I share Falo's opinion, I will not stop any of our hunters who may wish to assist our new allies." His golden gaze slides over Eral and his companions. "If you are all of the mind to go, I do not object, except to remind Eral that he has responsibilities here—so do not tarry too long hunting for the human."

Eral bares his teeth slightly but does not otherwise object to his alpha's command. He exchanges a look with the three other wolves and each of them nod to his silent question. He smiles coolly at his brothers.

"It is agreed. We will go then."

"I shall go as well," another female calls out, shifting the kit she holds to another female. She is large of size, larger than many of the other females of the tribe. "Cavek has been nothing but kind and generous to our kits in the days he has been here. I will not allow his mate and offspring to suffer without him."

Baru growls. "Shava, you would leave our kit? I forbid it."

Her ice-blue eyes narrow on him. "You forget yourself, mate. I am alpha of our tribe as well. If I choose to go, you have no command over me. Besides, our kits are weaned. They will be fine under my sister's watch."

It takes only a full day to arrive back at the palace of the Middling Way Kingdom. I do not even bother to go home. I do not wish to spend even a minute in that place so surrounded by the memory and scent of my mate while she's out of my reach.

Boukie flings her arms around me, her body wracked with sobs. My mother barely gives me a moment before she embraces me as well.

My mother, being a female of strong feeling, wears her sorrow like a heavy shroud. Almost literally. Not a single shiny bauble clings to her gown, and even the dress itself is the palest rose, lacking her usual vibrant edge. Concern seems to have infected everyone in the palace. Even my father's face is carved heavily with lines of worry. At his approach, anger flares up in me and I do not hesitate to slam my fist into his jaw. I hear a few of his teeth break.

The guards immediately shift their spears toward me, but the wolves converge around me, their fur bristling and lips pulled back from their fangs as they snarl threateningly. My father throws up his hand to halt the guard.

"Enough," he growls, an expression of remorse flashing over his face, and he rubs his jaw. "I deserved that."

"Uh, what?" I'm frozen in place as my father pulls me into a short hug.

"I did not think you had a hit like that in you, son," he says with a hint of pride. I almost want to snort derisively. It's not like I haven't beaten the shit out of plenty of people or killed my fair share in the heat of battle, but my father has always considered me softer in temperament compared to my brothers.

Still, I have never heard my father admit to any wrongdoing on his part.

My father clears his throat. "I may have been wrong to send you as a delegate without your family when you'd requested it."

Mother scowls. "Might have?" she snarls, her hair nearly standing on end. Father grumbles and shoots an annoyed glare at his mate.

"I was wrong," he amends gruffly. "You never would have taken them if you felt there was any danger. I shouldn't have insisted on your separation just because I thought your family might be a distraction. I apologize. I should have trusted your judgment. If I had, you may have been spared this loss."

I'm unwilling to accept any finality of 'this loss' that the rest of my family seems to be grieving over. They don't know my mate like I do. She will never give up, and she will protect our son. They're waiting for me to find them.

I accept the gruff condolences from Garol, and Mimi seems to be unable to stop crying. She gets her extreme sentimentality from our mother. Even though she only met Kate once, she's inconsolable. She soaks the shoulder of my tunic when we embrace. All of my family is present to be with me...

No, one person is missing.

"Cavek, I came as soon as I heard!" Vandra cries as she strides briskly into the room, the latest elvish fashion draping elegantly over her robust frame. It looks almost as ridiculous on her as mother's hideous attire, but I hold my tongue. I know that Vandra admires the elves, for whatever reason that may be. She's my sister and she's here for me, like always.

I smile and hug my sister. She smells peculiar, but Vandra spends a lot of time hunting and often comes home smelling strange. I frown as I catch the scent of blood.

"Vandra, did you hurt yourself?" I ask, pulling back to inspect my sibling.

"Nothing to worry about. We must focus on your mate right now," she says, trying to push me off. I grab her arm as she protests, but she gnashes her teeth with pain and shoves me back.

Boukie looks over at that moment, her eyes go wide, and she screams in panic as she clings tightly to Serus. Stitch, who'd been sleeping in a corner, goes berserk. Quicker than I have ever seen the lazy creature move, he's at our side and guards barely manage to restrain him when he attempts to lunge at Vandra. The entire room is in chaos.

I yank up the billowing sleeve of my sister's gown and stare in horror at the bandaging that wraps her arm from elbow to wrist. My heart sinks, even as my brain attempts to deny it. But there is no denying that she had been bitten by a young mawu—by Stitch.

"Vandra? You? Why?" I demand, my voice deepening with the snarl punctuating each word. "Why would you seek to destroy me?" I roar.

I leap at her with the full intent to end her miserable life right then and there as surely as she'd sentenced my mate and son to death without a qualm. My brothers barely manage to hold me back, even though they shake with rage themselves. None more than Serus, who stares in wide-eyed horror and disgust at our sister who has always been highly favored in our family and often spoiled.

"Destroy you? I have *saved* you. I have saved all of us!" she declares, her spine stiffening with pride. "When I overheard the elvish ambassadors tell Father that the elves would cut off any ties with us and refuse us entry into their territory or court if we took human mates, I knew I had to act. I couldn't allow it! She should have stayed gone. I stole her letter so that you would never know. I even arranged for the Warue to detain you so you could not return to Ov'Ge. You were supposed to forget her."

I look at her with disgust. I cannot believe this foul being is the one I've praised, loved, and called beloved sister for all these years. "*You* were the one responsible for my torture!"

She has the grace to look regretful at that. "I did not know that they would torture you—I swear it. They were just supposed to hold you."

"You gave them exactly what they wanted. A troll with access to our kingdom's secrets," I snarl. "What did you think they would do? And even that I might have forgiven, but you attacked my family? What did you do with them?"

Vandra straightens the hem on her sleeve and glares at me. "I did not kill them, if that is what you are asking. I merely dropped them deep in Warue territory. Those beasts can dispose of them however they see fit," she says with a dismissive wave of her hand as if my family was nothing to her but bothersome insects.

I roar in rage and again attempt to seize my sister. Only the efforts of both my brothers and the added strength of two werewolves keep me from tearing her throat out. I would delight to dance in her blood, to drench myself in it as a sacrifice to my mate should her shade already walk with her ancestors. All I can do is growl helplessly in the merciless grip of the males who restrain me.

"I will never forgive you for this, Vandra," I snarl. "I swear to you that if anything has happened to my mate and son, I will never give you a moment of peace, not even when your spirit departs for the next world. I will bind it so that I wreak my vengeance on you for the rest of days."

Vandra pales and steps away from me. She looks to our parents, her lip trembling.

"Mother? Father? You are not going to say anything?"

Mother takes a deep breath and steps forward with regal solemnity. She does not smile, nor does she laugh. She doesn't spare even a word for her eldest daughter. She looks her child in the face and swipes her claws down our sister's cheek, ruining not only her beauty but marking her for all to see as a betrayer of kin. She steps away and turns her back on our sister, gathering Boukie into her arms as she retreats from the room with a firm nod to Father as she departs.

"Father?" Vandra whispers.

Unlike Mother's unforgiving silence, Father looks genuinely pained. His usually stoic reserve crumbles and he seems to age right before me. The lines of sorrow become deeper grooves and he closes his eyes, the sparkle of moisture in his eyes the only indication of the true depth of his sorrow. He slowly regains control of himself and looks Vandra in the eye with steely resolve.

"Guards, imprison Princess Vandra," my father says with bitter resolution.

Vandra laughs. "Father, you cannot be serious. I heard you agree with an advisor that it would be best if we of the Middling Way not mate with humans rather than face the displeasure of the Sehriel court.

"That may be," my father agrees, his brow drawn low. "But once done, that did not mean I advocated doing anything that would harm your brother's mate or their bond, much less my grandchild. You have disgraced me and our kingdom, Vandra. You will be imprisoned for the rest of your days on the eastern border of our territory."

"Wait!" Vandra cries, her smiles yielding to a look of terror.

"Father no! I did it for you, for all of us. Father, wait!" she screams as the guards haul her out the door, the heavy doors slamming with finality behind them. It isn't until that moment that I am released.

I sag onto the floor, weeping bitter tears without shame. Mimi sinks down beside me and throws her arms against me, her soft face nestled beneath the roughness of my jaw. I feel a hand from each of my brothers rest lightly on my shoulders, giving comfort in their own way. I look up at them in gratitude. Serus is drawn and tired, but Garol surprises me the most. His usual reserved mask is shattered, and he looks down at me with raw compassion.

This betrayal has irrevocably changed all of us.

Shava comes up beside me, her ears flattened with concern. "That any female would think to give over another to the Warue Tribe…" she shudders. "Many of our females and kits have gone missing due to Warue raids into our territory. It is possible that they may keep her alive to get to you."

"So, we go into Warue territory and fight," Serus exclaims with a savage grin.

"It is not so easy as that," Eral murmurs, his left ear twitching. "The Warue have recently forged an alliance with the High-Ridge trolls and the hill ogres. They are monsters among us, giant brutes that will make terrible foes."

"Well then, we will get our own brutes," I say slowly, directing a knowing grin at Serus. "I think Sammi, the orc chieftain's mate, will be eager to know what has happened to her sister."

Eral slowly smiles.

My mind focuses on its deadly course. Orgath will help and, with our Evarue allies and troll magic, we will bring fury into the Warue territory the likes of which they've never seen.

CHAPTER 18

KATE

Cavekji whimpers in my arms and I do my best to comfort him. Although he's not the only baby in the cell, I try and keep him from disturbing the other females. The sunlight that filters in through a tiny carved-out window barely provides enough light to see anything more than dark shadows and shapes.

The females don't speak to me. They barely move from the corner they're huddled in together. I wouldn't even know they had babies among them if it weren't for the occasional glimpse of tiny furred bodies kept hidden in their midst. No one says anything except the high cries when a male enters to drag out a female from among them.

The females are pitifully thin. I don't think that most of them are members of this tribe of werewolves, given the state of their health. The newer additions are still robust, and their fur still has a sheen to it. A rail-thin gray female turns and looks my way, her yellow eyes shining in the dark. I watch in surprise as she uncurls from her spot and hesitantly approaches me.

Despite the thick pelt of fur on her back, shoulders and thighs, her belly and breasts have little more than the same gray peach fuzz from collar to pelvis. The fur on her head, however, is longer than my hair, lying in a thick mass down her back until it reaches her hip. It looks as ragged as the rest of her, with visible mats. Rather than multiple teats, which I would've assumed a female werewolf might have with their lupine anatomy, she has two round breasts on her chest like a woman, though her breasts hang from her emaciated form. She is bare except for the long sarong-style wrap around her hips that's seen better days. I can tell from hints of decorative embroidery and beadwork that it must have once been very fine.

Cavekji chooses that moment to let loose a full-throated wail and to my surprise she smiles and inches forward with her palms facing up. I watch her warily but nod when she indicates that she'd like to sit beside me. Her eyes don't move from my son as she lowers herself, her leg bumping mine.

"That trollbie, he is yours?" she rasps in a thin voice.

"Yes. This is my son, Cavekji."

She smiles and leans toward him, her eyes filled with sadness.

"Would you... like to hold him?" I ask.

The female's eyes widen for a moment but then she smiles her strange lupine grin and jerks her head in an enthusiastic nod. I settle him into her arms, and she snuggles him against her like a pro, her hand running over his fuzzy cap of hair.

"He is so sweet," she murmurs, giggling softly when Cavekji grabs ahold of a clump of hair and attempts to drag it into his mouth before she gently removes it from his fingers. "I had a kit, but he died. All of our kits are dying," she says, a tremor in her voice.

"Are you from the Warue Tribe?"

She shakes her head. "Not me, but there are several of their females in here with us. No one seems certain why they were culled from their tribe and placed in here. All I know is that they call this the female holding den. They say that they kidnapped us because their females keep losing their kits shortly after birth, but now those of us who have been stolen are suffering the same. They don't feed us anything but scraps nor allow us exercise and they wonder why we are fading away and the kits are dying," she snorts.

"That doesn't make any sense. If they wanted you for breeding, they would be feeding you enough to care for your kits and keep you healthy. Sounds more like they're setting you up for failure, so that no matter what happens, they have an excuse to get rid of you. But why would anyone want to do that?"

She shrugs morosely. "All I know is that the only time they take us out of here is to breed or dispose of us when we haven't satisfied them. Reya, the female taken earlier today, she lost her kit yesterday. She won't be coming back," she observes sadly. "No one will remember us so that we can join our ancestors."

"I'll remember you," I promise. And I will. If anything happens to her, I would never forget her.

Her lips twist. "Will you really? If you get out of here and I am gone, you will go and tell my living family and my ancestors at the ancestral shrine my name so that they will know me and remember me?"

"I promise."

She stares into my eyes and seems satisfied at what she finds there because she smiles. "I am Fahuri."

"I'm Kate," I reply, earning another quick flash of fangs.

Fahuri doesn't leave my side all day, nor the next. The other females start to migrate over. Their kits are so tiny and weak compared to Cavekji that I want to weep. They're listless and barely able to lift their heads. One of the females, a younger mother named Ahoa, whimpers with sorrow as her little one's head lolls, his little body laboring to survive.

She watches Cavekji nurse with sad eyes.

"All of my milk has dried up. They do not feed us enough. He is starving. I try to give him the mush the males throw in here, but he cannot hold it down," Ahoa cries bitterly. Many other females nod and echo her observation, their own babes fruitlessly rooting their withering breasts. The younger females among them have not yet whelped and watch on with sorrow.

Never in my life would I ever thought of putting another female's child at my breast, but it's not like there is formula on hand. Watching the kits struggle to survive pains me as a living being and as a mother. Finally, I pull Cavekji from my breast and ignore his angry protests as I reach toward Ahoa. Cavekji isn't going hungry, but her kit will die if I do not do something to help.

"Ahoa, I know we're not the same species and my milk probably won't be as good for him as yours is, but I'll nurse him while I can—if you will allow it."

The females stare at me in surprise and then Ahoa sets her hand on my arm with a relieved smile. "Among our kind, it is not odd for females to nurse for another when the mother is not present or is unable to. I would be so grateful if you would."

A tide of pleas rises from two other nursing females for help, and I assure them I'll do everything in my power to help. I take Ahoa's son, Meri, and prop him at my breast. At first, he doesn't respond, and I worry that he's too far gone, but a tiny drop of milk lands on his tongue and the kit lurches forward with what little strength he has and latches on.

It's startling at first, and it takes little to fill their tiny bellies. I move in quick succession onto the other kits to nurse them and return them to their mothers. Thankfully, my milk increase is slight but noticeable the next day. I've always overproduced milk whenever I nurse, both with Boukie and Cavekji, and it doesn't take much to kick it up a notch. Even so, I know it won't last long if we're stuck here too much longer. But it's something.

For two days, I feed Cavekji and the other three infants in the room, and we see nothing of any males other than the one who shoves scraps of food into the cell twice a day.

~

Cavek

It's the second time I am standing before Orgath looking for aide. Though it's an uncomfortable experience as he glowers at me from his throne, I am comforted with the knowledge that he doesn't hold me responsible for his mate's distress. And distressed is a polite way of describing Sammi at the moment. Orcs are known for their ferocity, but Sammi looks like she is ready at any moment to leap from her own throne and go kill someone.

I am all in favor of turning her against a few werewolves. It would be a sight to behold.

"Hill ogres," Orgath growls in disgust.

Of everything, that is what irritates him the most. Not that my mate is in the claws of werewolves. I am not entirely sure how I feel about it. Oh, it makes me angry, but I'm not sure if it is exactly because he considers the hill ogres a more serious threat. When it comes down to it, they are.

The Warue tribe could possibly have some compunction against killing my female, but ogres are known to be mindless beasts that kill with little provocation. I have to wonder what the wolves offered to make an alliance worthwhile.

Ogres are entirely male. There is only one thing of value that they could want. I stiffen as it finally comes to me. The Evarue Tribe has had females turn up missing. What if they are being traded to the ogres for their compliance?

The idea is too dreadful to consider and knowing that my mate is in the midst of that sends me into a killing rage of blood and darkness until I feel the biting grip of Orgath's large hand upon me. I come back to myself with Orgath's gray face just inches from my own, a snarl curling his lips as Sammi frantically tugs on him.

"Orgath! Let him go, you big oaf, and tell me what's going on! I know Cavek didn't just flip out for no reason at all. Somebody better tell me something, damn it!"

The male grunts and releases me, and my head hits the floor with a crack. I groan and cradle my head in my hands as I sit up.

"I can't believe you just did that," Sammi snaps.

"He is in one piece and alive," Orgath replies dourly, but then sighs. "The reason for concern, delfass-ki, is because they may be capturing females for the express purpose of gifting them to the ogres. Ogres are all male, so they use females from other species as breeders until the female is unable to bear young anymore. They are vile creatures," he spits out.

Sammi's mouth drops open. "And they have Kate? What are we waiting for? Thank the gods we've been working on swordplay. Let's go kick some ass!"

"You are not going anywhere, female," Orgath growls. "You will stay here with our child. I will call on Bodi and Ferli to help me assemble warriors to go with me to aid Cavek."

I watch as she narrows her eyes and her face flushes with anger.

"You're joking, right? I know you don't think you're going to just leave me here like some simpering princess in a castle tower. Do you have any idea how insulting that sounds? 'No, little female. Stay here and mind the little ones while the big strong man will go to battle.' I know for a fact that no orc female has to listen to that load of crap. Besides, Jake can watch her. You know he's not anything close to a fighter."

Orgath leans in to face his mate, his growl echoing around the common room of his keep, but Sammi doesn't even blink. She crosses her arms over her chest and juts her chin out with clear defiance.

Within hours, I am returning to the Middling Way with Orgath, Bodi, Ferli, ten strong orcs, and Sammi, clad in thick armor and wearing a shortsword strapped across her back and a half dozen knives at Orgath's insistence.

CHAPTER 19

CAVEK

I crouch down in the dense forest deep within enemy territory. Scattered all around me, hidden in the thick growth are my allies. The orcs grumble a bit as plants snag them. They aren't used to fighting in the dense growth of the forests of the Middling Way, but the Evarue have all but disappeared, melting into the foliage.

I lift my head from where I am sighting down an arrow and spy Garol in a tree with his bow drawn as well. He looks down at me with a vicious grin. I shake my head. The only time that male smiles is during battle. I feel sorry for his mate being joined to such a dreary male, but there must be something about him that she enjoys.

I twitch when Serus drops down by my side, his heavy sword balanced across his knees. He slaps my shoulder in a show of solidarity. I incline my head so that he knows I received his message. His smile widens and he creeps forward ahead of me to stop beside Orgath and Sammi. The female looks diminutive between them, but it gives me hope. Human females don't get the credit they deserve. Despite their fragile bodies, they are strong. My Kate will be alive and waiting for me.

Peering through the dense growth it is only by luck that I see Eral's dark ear twitch. Soundless, I relax my bow and slide over to him, but the male's ear turns toward me and he knows I'm coming before I even arrive.

"Where are they most likely to keep a captive female?" I whisper.

Eral grumbles for a moment in thought.

"Their dens are not set up like ours are. Normally, the families are kept closer to the center of the tribe with the single hunters or those pairs without young kits on the outskirts. We place our most vulnerable at the center to protect them. This tribe seems to be arranged specifically to a standard of hierarchy. Anything valuable they will likely set nearest to the alpha's den at the center."

I narrow my eyes and look at the dens constructed of mud and branches in the frame of the large root systems of the trees. One stretches out larger than the rest, and the large alpha goes in and out of it at regular intervals. That must be his den. I scan to the right and see a smaller structure with fewer windows than the other dens. I point the end of my bow toward it.

"What do you think? Seems a likely prospect."

Eral looks to where I'm pointing and nods.

"Yes, I would wager that to be the place where any females will be kept. It is close enough to the alpha where he can keep a direct eye on those coming in and out of it, and it is surrounded by the dens of the rest of the tribe. An arrangement like that not only protects them from outsiders coming in to steal the females, but it also prevents escape. It fits what we know of the Warue."

"Very well. I will inform Orgath and Serus."

I slip away from Eral's side and draw up beside Serus. He raises his brow at me and I point to the suspected den that may be holding Kate and hopefully some of the stolen Evarue females. Orgath observes silently on Serus's other side, but his eyes dart with a quick, analytical glances over the structures of the dens that surround our target area.

I still as the large bulk of an ogre moves into view. I've never seen one before and my breath lodges painfully in my chest. The ogre towers over even the largest of wolves by a good head, his sickly yellow flesh a disturbing sight. I am struck with horror by the very idea of a small female being brutalized by one of them. Orgath growls as several more come lumbering into view.

There is no doubt what the ogres are there for. We may have arrived just in time.

Orgath and Serus whisper to each other and Orgath raises his hand and cuts it through the air, summoning the orcs to blow the horns to alert everyone to advance. All around us, the horns erupt into a cacophony of trumpeting blasts, and the deep bellows of the orcs' war-cries merge with the roars of my brethren and the eerie howls of the Evarue. We surge forward as one through the dense trees and brush to slam into wolves that race to the perimeter of their den-grounds.

A small number of High-Ridge trolls emerge from their encampment just beyond the den-ground and run to meet us. They're distinct from the Middling Way trolls by their murky greenish-brown hue, white luminous eyes, and dark masses of hair. Their battle cry is the shriek of a wild cat, meant to strike terror. We collide with them, the crashing impact of bodies and armor ringing through the forest like an ominous death knell.

From my left, the Evarue burst forward and leap upon the Warue. Claws and teeth rip savagely into their targets as easily as my blade plunges into those enemies nearest to me. My battle lust mounts with every fatal wound I deliver and every head I sever from the flailing bodies. Hot sprays of blood hit me, and for the first time I relish it. For a second, I appreciate the enjoyment my brothers get out of battle, but for me this blood is sweetest because it's for my family.

Out of the corner of my eye I see Sammi thrust her blade through the throat of an imposingly large werewolf. A large ax swings out and decapitates another who attempts to protect its brethren. Sammi grins, a white slash through a mask of gore, and she looks at that moment as fierce as any orc. Orgath strides with his mate, covering her as they fight in a sort of synchronized dance, their bodies moving in choreographed steps.

An ogre rushes forward with a shout, his yellowing tusks encrusted with blood from where he obviously gored someone. He raises a huge iron-spiked club. Orgath steps in front of his mate, radiating fury as he faces the beast. Without hesitation, I spin close to the troll and slit his throat, releasing a wide-arcing spray of blood that I don't linger to relish.

Instead, I leap forward onto a fallen tree and yank an arrow out of my quiver. I force out a secretion of toxins from the glands in my throat. A bitter taste fills my mouth. I lick the arrowhead and notch the arrow, sending it flying into one of the eyes of the ogre. Blindness would normally only slow it down, due to the lower placement of the eyes away from the heavy boning that encases the brain inside its skull, but the toxin makes it roar out in agony.

The ogre stumbles, madly swinging his club, as Orgath and Sammi draw back and circle looking for their opening. It comes when Ethiel, their delfass, springs from the grass and its bulk collides with the ogre, tearing into him with a loud shriek. He leaps out of the way as the ogre rolls and that's when Sammi and Orgath attack. The female angles her blade to stab up under the bone-plated chest that protects its internal organs, disabling it long enough for Orgath to chop through its neck with two powerful swings of his battleax.

From my advantageous position perched as I am, I empty

my quiver before drawing my sword once more. I leap the short distance from the tree, slashing through the back of the Warue I fall upon. Blinking through the grime on my face, I narrow my field of vision onto the structure that I'm certain is holding my mate. Without mercy, I plow forward, sword in one hand and dagger in the other, eviscerating one male, my nose wrinkling at the scent of his warm guts dropping from his body. Another chokes on his own blood as I cut a gash into his neck.

I don't stop to finish the job or to give him a quick, merciful death. I don't stop in my onward push. My mate is a beacon calling to me, and I am pulled unfailingly toward her.

~

Kate

The loud noises from outside reverberate through the room, and I swear something huge crashes into the walls. Packed dirt from the mud walls shakes loose, baring roots in a manner that seems more than a little dangerous. Cavekji and the kits all start howling with a mixture of fear and displeasure. I clutch my son closer to my chest, curling my body over him.

"What the hell's going on out there?" I hiss as a bit of dirt gets in my eyes, making them water terribly.

"Ogres came today," Fahuri says. All the females shudder collectively.

"Is that a bad thing?" I'm not ashamed to admit when I'm clueless. Trolls and orcs didn't seem as bad as fiction paints them. Maybe ogres are just lovely too... even if that comes with terrifying earth tremors.

Ahoa nods, her face pinched tight. "Whenever the ogres

come, many females are taken. We don't know why, but every time the holding den is nearly emptied."

A shiver wracks my body, as icy dread crawls up my back.

"There are always problems when the ogres come. They are stupid and quick to anger. It is not unusual for there to be fights," a Warue female, Wavi, observes in a hushed voice as she cuddles her kit closer.

"What if it's the Evarue come to free us?" one of the newer females, Ethala, shouts excitedly. An enthusiastic buzz ripples among the Evarue females, but the Warue females seem to sink into themselves at the prospect.

"I hope so for your sake, but there is nothing to save us," Wavi sighs.

Fahuri narrows her eyes. "Ethala, do not encourage false hope. That can destroy us quicker than they can." She sets a comforting hand on Wavi and looks at the miserable Warue females. "As far as I am concerned, every female in this room is now Evarue. My brother is the alpha. I will see to it that you come with us if we manage to be freed."

Something changes among the females. A new kinship is formed with those few words. The Warue females merge among the Evarue, who warmly receive them among their numbers. They lean into each other's flanks in common sisterhood, taking comfort as the world rocks around us in a terrible clamor.

A shadow falls upon us from the opening and all the females stiffen. It's the guard. Krue is despicable. Although the alpha, Mercol, keeps him from touching any of us, he finds other ways to torment us. Masturbating in front of us and flinging his spunk at us is the worst of it when he isn't taunting us with detailed descriptions of what he'd like to do to us. For whatever reason, he enjoys torturing me with descriptions of the things that he did to Cavek during his time in captivity.

Never have I hated any living being the way I hate him.

He comes into the torch light and to my surprise he's wearing scaled armor. The scales wink in the light. I've never seen a werewolf wear any kind of armor in my time here, and I can't imagine why he'd choose to wear it now.

Krue ignores the other females. He's intent on me. He pushes his way into our cell, and the females who might have once attacked him when they were in good health scatter. A few bitches attempt to rush him, but he throws them to the side without breaking stride. Tears spring to my eyes when Ethala hits the wall with enough force that the crack of her neck breaking is audible.

A clawed hand jerks me forward out of the cell. I nearly drop Cavekji, but Fahuri comes to my aid and pulls him up into her arms, her expression filled with worry as Krue drags me to the other side of the cell. Both of my wrists are in one of his massive hands and he holds me far enough from his body to evade my kicks while he locks the cell behind us. Once he's certain the other females are secure, he draws my struggling body up close to him.

He leans his face into mine and his fetid breath hits me. I want to gag but settle for turning my head to the side. He chuckles and runs his nose along my neck.

"Sweet little female. It is interesting that I can still smell your mate on you. Even all these days apart, his scent has not weakened even a little. I like that. I will rut you with his scent clinging to you and know that I am vanquishing something that is his. I lost my right testicle to your mate, but now I will take something from him."

He turns me in his grip and shoves me against the wall, tilting my hips out. I scream as I feel his claws tearing at my clothes. I kick back and he laughs in my ear, his teeth nipping at my neck.

"Struggle all you like, female. If Cavek were here at this moment, he would tell you that I like it when my prey struggles."

Panic flares within my breast and I renew my fight. He curses when I throw my head back and by chance strike him square in the nose. A hand closes around my throat, applying just enough pressure for me to gasp for each breath. Cool air hits my bottom when he finally tears the lower half of my dress away. The females in the cell snarl and rage, but then a shocked silence settles into the room before a howl cuts through the air. Just as I feel his length slide against my ass, someone rips him away from me. A hot splatter of blood hits my back as I slide to my knees.

I slowly turn my head and the figure behind me panting over the body of Krue comes into focus. His emerald skin is painted over with crimson, and his eyes glow with a violent fire. That fire slowly dies away in his eyes and the return to the soft amethyst that I love so well. The familiar muscles of his arms sweep around me, pulling me against his rock hard chest.

"Cavek…" I whisper around broken sobs. "You're here."

"I will always come," he says, his voice thick with emotion. I wrap my arms around him and allow the horror of the last several days to melt away under his touch.

CHAPTER 20

CAVEK

I run my hands all over my mate, reassuring myself that she's okay. The foul odor of Krue is like a film over her skin. Never had I suspected he would survived my escape. I had hoped that he bled out and saved the world a lot of misery. If I had arrived even minutes later... I shudder at the thought of what almost happened. I allow my eyes to roam the length of her body, worry settling with a nauseating weight in my gut.

"Did he—?"

She shakes her head.

"He would have if you'd been any later, but this was the first time he tried," Kate says quietly. "The alpha kept him on a tight leash until now. He obeyed but he liked to cum on us, since that was the worst he could do."

I turn my face into her hair and breathe her in. The relief that fills me is staggering.

A lusty wail draws my attention. I turn my head and see a decimated female Evarue on the other side of the cell. The dyed tribal markings decorating her face are starting to fade with her time in captivity, but her tribe is unmistakable. Warue don't bother bestowing markings on their females. In her arms, Cavekji cries and struggles to break free from her grip. She offers my son to me with a shy smile.

I release Kate and open the cell, taking my son and pulling his tiny body close to me. Cavekji's cries die down to whimpers as he clings to my arm, several of my braids painfully tight in his grip.

I shudder with the realization of just how close I came to losing everything. It's likely that Kate would have been packed up with all the other females and given to the ogres if we hadn't arrived in time to stop to transfer.

My eyes flicker down to the male dead on the floor. His bowels hang all around him from the violence with which I'd gutted him. I feel nothing but satisfaction in his death. I hand my son over to Kate and lean down to remove my armor from his corpse. I'll be damned if his remains leave this world in possession of my favorite armor.

I unlash my breastplate and the simple leather armor from my body and let them fall to the floor. With the heel of my boot, I kick Krue over so that I can loot my dragon-scale armor from his body. Once it's free of his body, I slip it on and lash it over my frame. It stinks of the wolf, but I can ignore that for now until it can be cleaned.

The females slowly file out of the cell. Few still appear healthy, and I assume that these are the recent lost females, but the others are severally malnourished. What surprises me is that over half of the females—and those in the worst condition—are Warue females. They're so weak that they lean on each other. When a kit begins to cry, I see the tiny bodies for the first time, and I am sickened at the cruelty of the Warue. The female soothes the infant until it falls back to sleep.

The sounds of battle have died outside, and I can hear the

celebratory cheers and howls rising. I smile at the females looking around with confusion. Some wear a glimmer of hope on their faces. The Warue females look worried. I smile comfortingly at them.

"Come on. Let's leave this place. Warue, I swear no one will hurt you."

The female who'd held Cavekji straightens and looks at me sternly.

"There are no Warue in this room—only Evarue. This is so declared by Fahuri, first sister of the alpha and keeper of Evarue lore."

I incline my head with respect. "As you say then, Fahuri."

The females follow me without hesitation out of the holding den. The moment she breathes free air, Fahuri tilts her head back and lets out a delighted howl. The other females add their voices as it rises in a chain of harmony. Wolves from the battleground slowly add their voices to it. One by one, they arrive to greet the females.

First among them are Eral and Shava. Both come to a stunned halt in front of the den.

"Fahuri?" Eral whispers, his ears flattening as his eyes widen with shock.

"Fahuri!" Shava cries out happily, embracing the smaller female. Kate swallows back a happy sob as the females cling to each other. I pull my mate against my side, knowing well the happiness of reunion.

"Eral, Shava, let me introduce the new females of our tribe," Fahuri says with proud authority as she steps back to join the unmarked females. "Shava, I know it is ultimately by your grace that females are Evarue, but I ask that you not turn them aside. They have suffered enough already."

Shava blinks slowly as her eyes trail over them. Several of the females lower themselves to the ground, ears and tail low in submission. She suddenly smiles, and all the females visibly brighten.

"Stand, sisters. You are Evarue now, and we are one. You need not lower yourself to the dirt in front of me outside of ceding to a lost challenge. And from the state of you, none of you are going to be doing that any time soon," she says gently.

One of the unmarked females holding a kit laughs. She flinches as if the sound is foreign to her, but she returns the alpha female's smile.

"I do not think any of us will be challenging. We are all omegas, expendables among the Warue. We are happy enough just being a part of the tribe. We thank you," she says with a small bow.

The Evarue surround the females and I draw my mate and son away, my eyes scanning over the foliage that drips with blood. When I see the hulking frame of Orgath, I sweep my female up in my arms and rush over to deposit her right in front of her blood-bathed friend.

Sammi squeals with happiness, running forward to wrap her wet arms around Kate, holding her close. I step back beside Orgath to give the females space for the jubilant reunion. Even Orgath cracks a smile, his yellow eyes gleaming fondly at the embracing females.

Both Orgath and Sammi seem more mussed than I would have expected. They weren't just splattered heavily with blood, but in many places it is liberally smeared as if in the grip of some sort of frenzy. Recalling Sammi's liberation over a year earlier, I'm pretty sure I know exactly what the orcs were doing while I was retrieving my mate. The fact that the other trolls are studiously not looking at any of the orcs confirms my suspicions.

"Orgath, after the battle—did you—?"

He merely bares his tusks in a wicked grin. I promptly decide to 'shut the fuck up,' as my mate puts it. I really don't want to know any details of their post-battle activities, anyway. I lean against a tree, prepared to wait out the reunion of our mates.

A furious shriek rises alarmingly close when Vandra appears out of nowhere. She is disheveled from her escape from prison, her dress filthy and now stained from the battlefield. She raises a knife and leaps down at my mate with her dagger drawn. I stiffen and turn toward the females, knowing that I'm no longer close enough to intercept her.

My blood turns cold. Kate still has our son in her arms. She turns to look behind her, her face paling.

Energy crackles around us and tree roots spring from the ground, the sharp tips shooting out until they impale Vandra just inches away from my mate. Her eyes widen in a mixture of shock and pain, her knife falling from her fingers to the forest floor. Only one among us has that sort of magic. I look around until I see Mother standing nearby, her face a mask of sorrow, unmistakable even when wearing the signs of battle's labors. She approaches us, her mawu prowling behind her.

Vandra looks at her with hatred as she struggles to pull herself off the roots. It takes a lot to kill a troll. Even hitting a vital organ doesn't necessarily mean the end if one can hold on long enough to heal. It hurts like hell though; I can tell by the painful way she draws in air.

She summons enough within her to spit at Mother's feet.

"Ancestors curse you for harming your own blood," Vandra says weakly.

Mother shakes her head. "It is you who must now answer to the ancestors. Your father and I tried to be lenient and imprison you. We hoped that you would someday learn your error and make amends to the gods and ancestors who keep the Middling Way safe. You should have stayed in your tower. You left me no choice."

At Kate's side, my heart lurches as Mother turns her face

away and closes her eyes. I pull Kate and Cavekji into my chest. I do not want them to witness it, though there is little I can do to muffle what they will hear.

At Mother's sharp command, the mawu leap onto Vandra. Her body struggles as the first one bites down on her, and her painful gasps turn to screams that continue on and on until the last of her breath leaves her body and little remains but a mauled and bloody mess.

Mother blinks back hot tears but speaks for the benefit of the trolls who gather around us, having witnessed the attack.

"May the ancestors be satisfied. Vandra will not be buried or given respect by the living. We will forget her and her stain upon our family." Looking infinitely older, Mother hobbles away to rejoin Father at the edge of the battlegrounds. They turn amid their troops and mount their mawu to begin the journey home.

"She was responsible for all this, you know. For all of our pain," Kate says as she stares unflinchingly at what was once my sister.

I pull her back into my embrace, diverting her eyes, and rest my chin on her head. We stand there together, our son pressed between our bodies as he coos and gurgles without a care in the world.

"She was, but now she's nothing. Now, we forget her and take the best form of vengeance. We move on and live long happy lives."

CHAPTER 21

KATE

Stitch is going to be the most spoiled mawu in all of Middling Way. I decide this as I hold Boukie close to me. I hadn't imagined that Vandra would have gone after my daughter too until Cavek and Serus filled me on the events that occurred during my absence. Stitch saved my baby.

I'll never complain about that little beast again. Even when he shreds my favorite underwear.

"You shoulda seen it, Mommy. Stitch was scary! He got all big and made a scary noise. He bit the bad person, Mommy. He bit them and they ran away."

"Stitch is a very good mawu," I say, rubbing the scaly creature behind his large pointed ears. Stitch smiles up at me revealing all of his needle-sharp teeth in a typical doggy smile, his forked tongue lolling out with ecstasy as I hit a good spot.

I frown at the dry skin coming off his scales. It reminds me a bit of the shedding from a snake I had in my youth. I hope he's not sick. The last thing I need is Boukie's savior falling ill.

She's already telling everyone that he's her hero. She'd be devastated.

I hold up my hand with bits of his skin clinging to my fingertips.

"Cavek, is this normal?"

My mate comes over with Cavekji on one arm and peers down at my hand. He lets out a loud sigh.

"Yes, it's perfectly normal. Stitch is reaching his first growth."

"What does that mean?"

There's something ominous about the way he said that.

"He will experience a rapid period of growth, eat everything in sight, and smell bad from constantly shedding—which will also make a huge mess everywhere. This is why I didn't want a mawu."

"They sound like a teenage boy," I shrug nonchalantly. I remember Luke and Jake as teenagers. It was disgusting, but everyone survived just fine. "I doubt you'll love Cavekji any less when he gets to be a smelly adolescent."

Cavek grins toothily at me. "Perhaps, but by that age he will be going through exercise drills or beginning his apprenticeship under another troll when not studying with palace tutors, and I won't have to smell him all the time. I will just place warnings of high toxicity around his bedroom."

I snort out a laugh, but Cavek's grin only widens as he bounces our son.

"You think I am joking? You may think human boys are foul at that age, but a troll's venom glands start to develop as their sexual organs mature. Our glands produce both the sweet toxins for our mating bite and the bitter toxins we use to envenomate. It often secretes unintentionally, sweet when aroused or bitter when angry, and it mixes with our saliva until we have to spit it out. Adolescent trolls spit it out wherever they happen to be. If it's not cleaned up, it will reek after a short time," he laughs.

"That. Is. Disgusting."

"But you will not love him any less," Cavek says playfully, turning my own words back on me. He settles onto the seat beside me and I immediately take the opportunity to lean into his side, relishing the comfort of being pressed up against him.

Cavek goes out later in the evening on his patrol through the villages assigned to him on his daily route. I know he prefers the night shift because it gives us the most time together during the day, and he knows that I will often wait up for him to return. The only downside is that I usually have to put the kids to bed by myself, and sometimes Boukie can be a real handful to put down. This evening, however, Serus came over to play with her, which has made the evening far easier for me to manage.

Serus shoves a sandwich I made out of dried fish and about the closest thing I can manage to mayonnaise into his mouth. It tastes a little off—but not too bad. Much to my amusement, the guys love it. I have to make no less than three sandwiches to keep up with one male troll's appetite for a snack. As I watch Serus put away yet another sandwich, a thought occurs to me.

"Serus, how come I've never met your mate?"

He shrugs good-naturedly. "We have an agreement. We mated to keep our families happy, but we do our own thing. Sometimes she will feed me if I show up at the right time," he says with a laugh. He must have noticed the look of horror on my face because he adds, "It works well for us. It got exhausting having Mother set up a parade of females every week as if it were entertainment arranged for market day. I would much rather spend my evenings playing with Boukie than going through that nonsense to look for a mate I may or may not find."

His shrug is so pragmatic I decide to drop the subject. Cavek should be arriving home any minute, and then—sorry, Serus—I'm kicking his brother out. I prepare another three sandwiches for

Cavek and set them on the table. Serus immediately reaches for them and I slap his hand. He shoots me a look of betrayal.

"You had yours, greedy. These are for Cavek."

"Cavek gets to eat good every day. I am allowed to wither away unless I go to the palace or come here. If I ate these, he would never miss them," Serus says pitifully.

I roll my eyes.

"You and I both know you're not in any danger of starving. You eat more than any two grown human men, but I feed you anyway. You already ate. Now hands off."

"Be off with you, Serus," Cavek says cheerfully as he walks through the door. I didn't even hear him approach. Even after all these months together, he still can sneak up on me. Trolls must be part ninja. Well, everyone except Serus. He lumbers like an orc. I look speculatively between the brothers.

"Cavek, are you sure you two are related and he isn't a half-orc foundling?"

My mate winks and snatches up his plate in time to prevent his brother from pilfering his sandwiches. Undeterred, Serus laughs and throws himself against the back of his seat, stretching out his long legs. He scratches at his jawline.

"I am going to miss this," he says with such feeling that I look at him puzzled. I don't think he means he's going to miss it while he takes his turn at the territorial perimeter patrol. Serus's eyes flicker to Cavek.

"You haven't told her yet?"

"Not yet," Cavek says. He polishes off the first of his sandwiches with just two bites. "I just heard today before my patrol."

"Told me what?" I ask anxiously, looking back and forth between them.

"Cavek here is being officially made Middling Way ambassador to the orc clan under Chieftain Orgath. He will return for a few weeks in the midsummer to celebrate the turn of the year and report to Father and allow you all to enjoy the festivities, but otherwise you will be living among the orcs. May the gods have mercy on you," Serus teases.

My mouth dropping open, I turn to Cavek. "Really? We'll be living near Sammi?"

Cavek nods and shoves the rest of another sandwich into his mouth before opening his arms to catch me as I leap on him. I wrap my arms and legs around him, dropping kiss after kiss all over his face. I feel his cock against my core and he captures my lips turning the kiss to something more intimate.

Serus chuckles and moves toward the door.

"I think your mate is happy, brother. I think I will leave now before she appreciates you a little too thoroughly and scars me for life."

Cavek waves his brother away with one hand as he plunders my mouth, his tongue sliding upon mine. The door shuts firmly behind Serus. At that sound, both of Cavek's hands drop from my waist to cup my ass as he begins to grind against me. I moan into his mouth.

"Are we going to make it into the bedroom?"

"Are the kids asleep?" he asks, doing a delicious swivel against me.

"Gods, yes."

"Fuck the bedroom," he grunts and flips me so I'm leaning over the table.

I push back against him eagerly, rubbing against his cock pushing out of his breeches as he fumbles with the hem of my dress. Once he has ahold of it, he shoves it up over my hips, baring my ass and pussy to him. Without hesitating, he falls to his knees and licks me from clit to ass with sweeping strokes of his tongue. I choke on a strangled cry of desire.

His mouth moves over me with the expertise bred of familiarity with my body, pulling moans from me with every long lick and teasing nibble. His lips gently tug on my folds that are swollen with desire. He pauses every now and then to plunge his tongue deep within me, drinking from me like a male dying of hunger and thirst. And my mate is ravenous. My back arches as an orgasm rips through me, fireworks popping in my blood as fresh heat floods my pussy. Cavek growls against my flesh and laps it up greedily until nothing remains. Only then does he finally pull back and look at me. I see little more than the glow of his eyes in the rapidly dimming light.

He breathes a word that snaps with power and small lights leap up on their sconces along the walls. The only thing that doesn't light is the hearth, and I thank the gods for that because as summer solstice nears it's only getting hotter and more humid.

I lay my head back against the table and tilt my hips as I feel his cock nudge my slick folds. I'm more than ready for him. The two small knobs of his piercing and the pebbly texture of his skin brush against my sensitive skin as he slowly sinks into me. After days apart my body resists ever so slightly, but it makes the burn all the more exquisite. We moan together when he bottoms out in me. To my surprise, he doesn't move. Instead, he leans forward and rests his head against my shoulder, his breathing ragged.

"I don't think I am going to last long," he grits out apologetically.

"Then you'd better fuck me hard and quick," I reply, swallowing back a moan as his cock twitches deep inside of me.

Cavek snarls and latches onto my throat with his teeth. The sensation is almost familiar to the night we mated, except he doesn't break skin. He only restrains me. His hands grip my shoulders and I feel his shaft withdraw from my body. The wet squelching of my pussy is loud as my body attempts to keep him deep within me. He pulls out to the tip and I whimper before he rams himself home again. My knees bump into the table as my body lurches forward, but I'm kept in place with his unbreakable hold.

In and out he shuttles, my pussy wetter with every brutal thrust, my breasts swinging until he lets go of my shoulders to cup them with his large hands. His fingers pull and pluck on my nipples, teasing my nerve endings. I feel each tug in the very core of me, tightening until it spills over into an orgasm. But that's not enough for him.

Cavek releases one breast and allows his hand to slide down, dipping over my stomach until he reaches the apex of my thighs. On his next forward lunge, he wedges his hand between my legs to cup my mons. One finger carefully slips over my clit, rubbing it relentlessly as he rides me. I feel the world go out of focus. A tremor sweeps through me like riding the highest crest of a wave as I feel him swell within me. Then everything inside me shatters and my pussy squeezes him as he pulsates and drenches my insides with his copious seed.

We collapse together on the table until I shove him off me so I can breathe. He mutters an apology and pulls me over his chest, our hearts both beating out a rapid tempo. Everything gradually comes back into focus. I'm pretty sure he just fucked me cross-eyed for a moment there.

I wince and sit up slowly.

"Okay, maybe fucking on the table—as sexy and spontaneous as that sounds—was a really bad idea," I groan.

Cavek stretches his back and climbs off the table to fetch a damp rag, which he sweeps between my legs and down my thighs before wetting it again to clean his cock.

That's one thing I can really brag about: my mate keeps his shit clean. No nasty mystery smells coming from there and very little ball sweat odor unless he's been laboriously working on something. While I imagine drying semen isn't comfortable, I know it's really a courtesy to me, one that I greatly appreciate.

After ogling him for several minutes and admiring that nice male part that just turned my world upside-down, I wrangled my brain long enough to form intelligible conversation.

"We're really going to the orc village?"

His lips curve and he nods.

"Father knows that diplomacy is where my interest lies. I'm not like my brothers, who happily look for an opportunity to fight and find patrolling to be fulfilling work. Not that I don't enjoy beating on someone every now and again. Don't get me wrong. I am a troll, after all," he says with a disdainful snort. "But I want more than that, and I think that the Middling Way needs ambassadors. I've been advocating for it for years. Father agrees now that he's seen the true strength of allies."

I bound up in excitement.

"This is fantastic! I can't wait to tell Sammi. Wait… when are we leaving? Will she even have time to receive a letter?"

Cavek chuckles. "We still have a few weeks left. We won't be departing until after the High Sun Festival. Plenty of time to ready our family for moving and enjoy the festivities of the season here."

I drape my arms over his shoulders and feel the silly grin as it spreads on my face.

"Still going to take me to the lotus pond for the pixie orgy?"

His smile widens with a touch of mischief. "Pixie-dust-induced sex? We can't miss that."

I giggle and hug him close to me. I can't believe it. I have my family and soon I will be together with Sammi again. Things can't get any better than that.

CHAPTER 22

KATE

The High Sun Festival is beyond anything I would have imagined. The entire clearing is lit by pixies flitting through the air. But what's truly captivating are the performers who are everywhere.

Boukie has Cavek and I each by the hand, dragging us through the small market area. She jumps back as a fire-breather blows fire out of his throat just feet away from us without a torch. Troll magic is subtle, and they seem to use a lot of it for amusement. Boukie giggles and claps her hands.

I smile and lean to the side to whisper to Cavek. "Correct me if I'm wrong, but as far as I've seen these last few months, including on the battlefield, most examples of troll magic either involve subterfuge or entertainment rather than anything… uh… big."

Cavek snickers, his sexy lopsided smile baring his fangs. "That is an accurate—if not simplistic—summation of troll magic. Some more industrious among us will study the more powerful spells, but most don't have the patience or interest to go through all that. Father learned just enough magic to seduce Mother, but she is one of the most powerful trolls in Ov'Gorg."

I raise my eyebrows. "What magic did your father learn to win your mother?"

He smirks and adjusts the baby sling draping across his chest.

"He gave Mother a flower bud brought from the gardens of the dryads. It was her favorite flower and very difficult to get. He set this dried bud in Mother's hand and made it bloom right there. He said that was the only bit of magic that he ever found worth the trouble of learning since she agreed to mate him that night."

I rest my head against Cavek's arm.

"You know, that's actually really romantic."

Cavek tilts his head thoughtfully. "That's what Mother says whenever she tells the story. Speaking of—there she is."

I look over and to my not-surprise she's introducing a young troll, of a forest green hue, to an apple-faced female who gleams a lovely shade of jade. Ah, Madi. Although she's not fully back to her old self as far as I can tell, she seems in good spirits doing what she loves to do: interfere in people's love lives. I choke back a laugh as a mischievous smile spreads across her face and she "accidentally" shoves the bashful youth into the female.

They flail and fall over as Madi feigns horror. She apologizes but the experienced individual can see the gleam in her eye that belies her words. The male jumps to his feet and in a rushed apology helps his love interest back up out of the dirt. The dismay at her festival dress being ruined is fleeting, and she smiles at his efforts to dust her off and win her over with a cool treat. Madi looks nothing less than smug as they wander off arm-in-arm.

Cavek makes a disgusted noise in the back of his throat.

"Now that Mother has run out of children to play matchmaker to, she's set herself loose over the rest of the populace. How horrifying."

"I think it's cute," I say, shoving a bit of spun sugar—that's similar to cotton candy but even better somehow—into Cavek's mouth to silence him. He grins around the confection and licks it off his lips in such an intentional way my belly heats.

"Behave," I whisper, swatting at him.

My eyes track Boukie as she wanders over to a low stage surrounded by trollbies and children of various species attending the festival. There are even a few orc children mingled among them, since Orgath and Sammi have come with a number of orcs in a show of friendship. The children fall silent as a number of tiny magic flames spring out around the perimeter of the stage.

An elderly troll walks out onto this stage. He's possibly the oldest troll I have seen yet. His dark green skin is creased with wrinkles, and his lavender hair has gone completely white and hangs down in a tangled mass. When he speaks, though, his voice is a deep baritone with only the slightest rasp to betray his age. As he spins his stories, he weaves simple illusions with his magic to accentuate his tale. He's so captivating that even adults stop to watch. This goes on for well over an hour, one tale slipping into another until the elder bows and retreats from the stage.

Boukie comes running up, her face radiant. She's holding hands with the boy from the palace. The small male appears to be completely smitten with Boukie, willingly allowing her to pull him around to whatever destination she spontaneously sets her heart on. He appears to be two or three years older than her, but that doesn't concern me. He obviously dotes on her. Rather, I worry for him. Boukie can be a beast at times. No doubt he is aware of that fact and is still looking at her like she's the best thing since sliced bread. I'm glad she has a devoted friend like that.

Cavek examines him, the corners of his lips quirking despite the fierce glower he attempts to adopt. Although he isn't Boukie's biological father, though I have no doubt that the man who gave her life would approve of Cavek, he plays the overprotective daddy role very well.

"Who is this?" he grumbles.

"Daddy, you know who he is," she giggles. "Uncle Serus told you. He's my friend Bafulk."

"Boukie, even if he knows, it's still polite to introduce him," I remind her gently. Boukie is slow to grasp manners, but that's normal for kids her age back in the human realm. "Now try again."

Boukie lets out a put-upon sigh and whispers, "This is stupid," but plasters an eager to please smile on her face when I narrow my eyes at her. Seven years old is too young for an attitude like that. I dread puberty if she's already getting this mouthy. What ever happened to my sweet little girl?

"Daddy and Mommy, this is my friend, Bafulk."

"It's very nice to meet you, Bafulk" I say kindly. Cavek is silent beside me, obviously still sizing up the male. I nudge him with my elbow, which my mate doesn't even acknowledge. To my surprise, the child bows so far that he nearly prostrates himself.

"Forgive me. I didn't protect Boukie and she was almost hurt. As her friend and a male, I failed."

I blink at the rather formal speech coming from a child. Cavek, however, appears unmoved as he frowns down at the trollbie. His critical gaze sweeps over him and the youth almost appears to wilt.

"Cavek," I hiss. "Be nice to her friend."

My mate mumbles something unintelligible under his breath, but he smiles and inclines his head in polite greeting.

"No harm done, Bafulk. You attempted to intercede to the best of your abilities. You showed bravery despite the odds. You are proven and your name is noted."

The boy relaxes noticeably and puffs out his chest with pride. He smiles with such pleasure one would think he'd done something pretty grand. The two of them scamper off while I'm still busy trying to work out just what exactly happened here.

"Okay, what did I miss?"

"Nothing aside from the fact that you rushed me through one of the pivotal moments of that trollbie's life," Cavek complains half-heartedly.

"You're going to have to break that down for me, because I don't see how I did any such thing. That boy was clearly terrified of you."

Cavek rolls his eyes. "No, he wasn't. Not really. He was more anxious because, despite his failings which he acknowledged, it's an important landmark for him." I continue to stare at him with full-on cluelessness and he sighs.

"When a male trollbie gets to be around the age of ten, they have their first hashavan rites. This means they must get approval from the father of their closest unrelated female acquaintance that they are seen as a worthy companion. A male who doesn't pass this milestone will have difficulty as he gets older when he attempts to court females. Trolls are a gossipy bunch, and everyone will know if he failed to get that approval. No doubt because he'd attempted to protect Boukie, his family decided that it was the best time for him to fulfill his hashavan."

Both my eyebrows shoot up. "That's pretty intense." Maternal alarms immediately start blaring through my psyche. "Wait, that doesn't mean he's courting her, does it? They are too young!"

Now he laughs.

"No, love. A troll won't have much interest in bonding before he is at least an adolescent, and I doubt it is that much dissimilar with humans. They are just friends, which is the most necessary part of his hashavan. It merely demonstrates that he is worthy of trust for the welfare of an unrelated female. It's a test of his character."

"Isn't ten a bit young to determine that? I don't want anyone judging my son when he's ten on the matter of his character based on the say-so of some little girl's daddy. That's not fair."

Cavek rubs a soothing hand on my arm, but his body shakes with silent laughter, which irritates me even more.

"Don't stress over it. Bafulk got off easy. Usually there is all kinds of quizzing and demonstrations, but unless a male shows a deciding lack of character, they always gain the approval. They are just made to sweat a bit. Here in about a week's time I will go to his hashavan ceremony and confirm him in front of his kin. Boukie was clever to wait until the High Sun Festival to introduce him, likely wagering on the public venue to dissuade me from making the process a lengthy one."

"I still think ten is too young to decide such things," I mutter.

"Trolls reach adolescence at the age of roughly thirteen. Should they be made to wait until then, when they have hormones running wild through their bodies? A young troll male is uncontrollable at that time in his life. The hashavan is more psychological, keeping the male grounded by his socially recognized responsibilities. At ten, males are feeling the desire to take on responsibility without the burden yet of hormones influencing them at every turn."

"I suppose that makes some sort of sense," I agree reluctantly. "How did your test go?"

Cavek shudders. "Terrible. Asana was a female who my mother arranged for me to befriend. I don't make friends quickly and she didn't want me to 'fall behind' in my tests among our kind. Her father quizzed me for two hours in the hottest room of his den until begrudgingly giving me his approval. Most miserable experience of my life, especially when Asana saw no need to continue our friendship afterward."

"Brutal."

"That's the problem with having a romantic for a mother. She is convinced all she needs to do is put people together in the right conditions and they will just click. She'd assumed that arranging for me to have an appropriate friend would mean that we would be friends," he says with a laugh.

"Well, that explains Serus..." I mutter.

Cavek frowns down at me, pulling Cavekji's hand out of his face as our son stretches his tiny limbs.

"Explains what? Start talking, Kate."

I bite my lip. I didn't mean to let that one slip, but how was I to know that Serus kept his brother in the dark over his mating?

"Serus happened to mention that he and his mate are only together to keep your families from constantly trying to interfere in their lives. They live together, but otherwise they lead completely separate lives."

"That doesn't make sense. I have seen them together. They act as any mated couple..."

"All choreographed to make it believable, I'd guess."

∽

Cavek

Knowing that my brother is living a farce of a mating makes me all the more grateful for finding my bloodbonded mate. I knew that he wanted to escape Mother's constant nagging, but it's beyond incredible that he felt the need to establish a false mating.

It is sad. More than that, it is dangerous.

Lies and deceptions of such magnitude eventually blow up in the face of the one who hides behind them.

Kate's small fingers entwine with mine and I shove aside the weight of my concern. There's nothing I can do about it. What my brother and his mate have done will eventually need to be dealt with. But that's not something that anyone else will be able to do

THE TROLL BRIDE

for them. Instead of dwelling on it, I turn my attention back to the festivities going on around us.

The High Sun Festival is something that everyone in the Middling Way looks forward to all year, and many neighboring species travel just to take part. We suspect that the pixie mating season is the draw. While most lotus ponds are in private territories near our dens, there are a few public ones that the adventurous visitor can take advantage of.

The satyrs in particular enjoy it. Satyrs are extremely lusty creatures and put themselves at strategic spots near the public ponds to seduce any female who is hit by pixie dust. I eye a small group of five males prancing in a sexually provocative dance to a flute barely visible outside of the designated family area. We trolls are not shy about our sexuality but once satyrs started showing up, we decided collectively that there were just some things not everyone needed to see.

Kate chooses that moment to crane her neck to see what I'm looking at and promptly turns away red-faced.

"That was a bit of an eyeful," she mutters to herself.

I press my lips together to keep myself from laughing. My poor female, despite much of her boldness, is uncomfortable with such displays.

"Please tell me that they aren't going to be hanging around the lotus pond."

"Not our pond, anyway," I agree with a quick smile.

"But at the public ones, I take it. I sure hope all the females around here got the notification."

I watch a female werewolf approach one of the satyrs with a keen interest in her eye and her thick tail flagging, and I chuckle.

"I suspect there are going to be enough females intentionally showing up that there won't be any problems."

As we wander among the stalls set within small clearings between the thick growth of trees and the path of streams, my mate exclaims over nearly everything she sees. The dryads draw Kate in to dance with them and several other females for a while. We then spend quite a bit of time listening to the haunting singing of a trio of mermaid sisters who have traveled all the way from their cove to celebrate the high sun with us.

These sisters come every year, although sometimes they arrive with others of their kind to perform together. One of the females who recognizes me waves and blows me a kiss, much to my embarrassment. I cling to my mate in a clear warning. The mermaid merely winks, although I'm pleased to see her falter when my mate attempts to advance on her. My heart swells with love but I restrain Kate. Mermaids may look soft and sweet like humans, but they are not. Male merfolk are okay, but the hot-tempered females will chew someone up and spit them out with little provocation.

I do discover that Kate is particularly interested in some of the enchantment tournaments and the mock battles. Although I do suspect that with the latter, she just enjoys watching the half-naked males show off their strength. Much to my amusement, Serus and Orgath compete against each other, and Sammi yells louder from the sideline to support her mate than anyone else in attendance. It provides almost as much entertainment for those gathered as the contest itself. I hug Kate close to me to remind her just who her male is before I redirect her attention to something else that she finds pleasing. I'm not jealous—much.

We do not see much of Boukie since she spends most of the day with Bafulk and his family, although occasionally the pair will trail along with us before running off again to play a game or look at some craft or display. Even Cavekji seems to be in a good mood throughout the day when he is not dozing. At some point, Kate gives him a peach to suck on and within twenty minutes I'm wearing the juices and the mashed remnants of the fruit.

When evening nears, we run into Orgath and Sammi again.

Or, more accurately, we run into Orgath. We find him standing outside a large stall bouncing his daughter, Ferona, in his arms, who's wide-eyed and jabbering away in her broken baby talk despite the late hour. I don't even have to ask where Sammi is, because every so often he glances into the stall with a look of resignation and love on his face. She rejoins him just as we draw up beside him. Sammi shifts her bundle in her arms and plays with Cavekji.

"Where's Boukie?" she asks, as she makes a ridiculous face at my son.

"A few booths down looking at enchanted blades," I say.

"Excuse me, she's *what*?" Kate says as she slowly looks up from cleaning our son's face.

"No one is going to sell her an enchanted blade," I laugh. At least I'm fairly certain they won't. "Besides, I already told them she had to wait until she is at least fourteen years old. We don't give minors weapons."

Kate's eyes widen further. "You consider fourteen to be an adult?" she asks wanly.

I scrub the back of my neck. "Not exactly, but we do consider them of age for apprenticeship at that time, which often involves training with tools and weapons depending on what they are doing. We call that the apprentice stage. It's between minor and adult."

My mate rubs her face and groans and Sammi giggles and rubs her back with sympathy.

"Hey, don't worry. It's not all that bad. Orgath has already started building an arsenal for our daughter for when she comes of age."

"It is good to be prepared. She will have all that she needs for her training," Orgath says simply as he allows Cavekji to play with his thick fingers. Ferona stares down at Cavekji with total fascination, which he returns. They both giggle and grab at each other.

"Looks like they just might be great friends already," Sammi says. She looks at us speculatively. "You guys look like you could use some quiet time. Tell you what, why don't we take Cavekji and Boukie off your hands? Knowing Kate, she has extras of everything the kids need packed in the diaper bag. We need bonding time with the little guy, anyway, since you're coming to our village soon."

Kate and I exchange a look, and I see relief and a burning need hidden in her eyes. Their spark of promise starts a fire kindling within me and I find myself eagerly handing my son over to our friends.

"Just be careful with him," I caution as I hand his sling and baby bag over. Orgath rolls his eyes but Sammi giggles.

"Relax, Cavek. Orgath and I survived the baby days and have another on the way," she says, patting her slightly rounded belly.

"Gods help us all," Kate chirps. Sammi bursts out laughing.

"Go, both of you, before we change our mind," she threatens as she cuddles our son. The last thing I see as Kate pulls me away is Ferona grabbing a handful of Cavekji's hair and pulling.

"Kate, don't you think—"

"Cavek, I do believe you promised to take me to our lotus pond. The pixies are all gone from the festival. We're going to miss the good stuff!"

I laugh and allow my mate to tug me down the path toward our home.

CHAPTER 23

KATE

The pond in the fading light is brighter than I've ever seen it. Everywhere, dozens of pixies are flitting, so much so that it brightens the air. Even the light mist that's rolled in is turning shades of pink and purple from the glow of the females. The males, however, are easily a hundred smaller lights dancing around them.

There are obviously many more hives of males than there are females to queen them. The hopeful males zip around in arcing, dancing displays in an attempt to entice the attention of a female they desire. The females flutter lazily around the flowers, showing off their large bright wings.

After what seems like something caught between a breath and the rolling endless march of time, the females ascend from the pond, carrying nectar in small bowls from the lotus blooms. Time has no meaning; everything is eternal and there is something so profound and mystic at this moment. Far more powerful than the aphrodisiac dust. Perhaps others come for this feeling of eternity and ancient power that I am feeling. And at this moment, I'm pretty sure I'm drugged by the pixie dust.

It starts so slowly that I barely notice at first until it gathers like ultra-fine pollen in the air, shimmering pink "dust" drifting through the air. I watch as it slowly starts to gather on my skin. At first, it's just a few flecks, like freckles. But in no time, it looks like I spent the afternoon playing in glitter.

As the dust builds, a tingle washes over my skin that slowly seeps into my blood like a warm caress. It licks through me, gaining power the more the pixie dust coats my skin. My heart beats quicker and to my surprise I feel the first quiver of interest from my sex. I clench my thighs together and swallow back a moan as the sensation rises.

Looking over at Cavek, his green skin covered with the glowing pink dust makes him sparkle like an exotic gem. His eyes burn with desire and his cock bulges against his breeches, and I know he's just as affected as I am. His pupils are blown out with desire, and he clenches and unclenches his hands in forced restraint. He's teetering on the edge of civility.

He licks his lips as his eyes rove over me, and fresh wet heat soaks me under the perusal. All he has to do is look at me and I'm a needy mess. To my embarrassment, I'm so aroused, so wet, that I feel a trickle of moisture run down my inner thigh. Cavek's nostrils flare and he growls deep in his throat.

"Cavek," I whisper, my voice weak with longing.

Like a predator faced with vulnerable prey, he doesn't waste any time. I'm barely aware of his movement soon enough to open my arms for him when he's upon me. We collide and fall into the mossy slope near the pond. His mouth crashes down upon mine and a guttural growl rises ceaselessly from within him.

I find myself responding to that primal sound as I pull at his clothes with eager hands. Impatient, he stands up and strips in a rush before falling upon me again. His claws carelessly tear open my clothes, and my breast spring out into the open air as my pussy throbs.

Gods, if this can make me feel this eager every time, he can demolish my clothes any time he wants.

~

Cavek

Desire is an inferno within me. Never before had I willingly exposed myself fully to pixie dust the way so many others do. It's a shock to my senses, but I do not think I would feel so strong if it wasn't experienced with my bloodbonded. Coated with this pixie dust, she shines bright as a star. A living star gifted to me that I may hold, love, and adore. Almost unable to believe she's real, I breathe her in deeply. My hands stroke her body, stoking the burnishing flame of her arousal until that's all I'm aware of.

I can't get enough of her. Her scent, already the sweetest to me, pulls me in and drowns me in pleasure. I am helpless to resist. Everything I love and adore about her is magnified by the pixie dust. Her hair gleams with highlights of blue and purple in the pixie lights and it coils around my arms like a lover's caress. Her lips are red from my kisses and all I want to do is drink from her until I am satiated.

I marvel at the softness of her skin, so sweet against my tongue as I lick the stain of my mark that brands her shoulder, and she quivers in my arms like a leaf in autumn. So, I nip lightly at it and her body arcs into mine, pressing against the length of me with her silent demands. These I am eager to obey.

Every bit of my instinctual drive clamors at me to bury myself within her and release my seed. To fuck her until I don't have energy to do anything but lie panting in the grass.

My fingers rub the small nub of flesh between her legs and slick through her folds, diving into the warm, hot grip of her until wetness floods my hand and she sighs. It's a long moaning sound that wracks my body with pleasure. This moan turns ragged, and she begins to pant and shiver with another orgasm as I relentlessly push her into another. I can't wait any longer.

I pull my fingers free from her most intimate place and sit back on my haunches. I move Kate into my lap as I suck her tongue into my mouth. My cock is so hard it aches, and my balls are heavy. Pulling her thighs to either side of me, I lift her and without error line her cunt up with the head of my shaft before pulling her down on me with desperation.

When her ass meets my legs, I rock against her, grinding into her. I lock my eyes with hers and marvel at the shine of pixie lights reflected in their beautiful depths. I lift her up and drag her back down again. She whimpers and it blends in with the humming sighs of pixies mating in the air around us.

A female and her three males flit by us. Two of the three males are in a breeding lock with her, and I recall enough lore to know that they are pumping into the female's cunt at the same time while the other male waits for one to drop off so he may take his turn to breed. Although I have no desire to share my female, for some reason it stokes my own lust as a fresh coating of dust falls from them upon us.

With vigor, I lift my hips and thrust up in time as I slap her ass down on my thighs. She wiggles and cries, her breasts jiggling, her thighs gripping me, and her toes digging into the mossy grass. Kate winds her arms around my neck. I whisper her name and mine bursts forth from between her lips in a sigh of ecstasy.

Our movements become sharper as I jerk her down upon my hard length. Her cunt grips me with every quiver, and every rippling orgasm attempts to draw my seed from my body.

I reach up with one hand, the other grasping her hip, and

THE TROLL BRIDE

tangle my fingers in her hair, drawing her head back to expose her throat. I lick her from collar to jaw and back down again before biting on the soft flesh at the side of her neck. Kate shrieks and her silky sheath bears down on me. Her nails scrape over my back.

It's too much. My cock swells as I rock it within her tightening sex. It pulses and then I roar as the power of my release shoots down my back and thighs, and my seed jettisons into her until I have nothing left to offer to my mate.

Spent, we lay together, belly-to-belly. Kate is on my chest and I close my eyes and enjoy the feeling of her breath moving through her body, even though we're both slick with sweat, her juices, and my seed. Dirt clings to that concoction but I can't be bothered to care. The last lights of the pixies drift away from the pond. The new families have retired, and those males left wanting are returning to their hives to try again next year.

Kate's finger traces unfamiliar patterns along my skin, and I suspect she's also watching the last fading flickers of the pixie dance.

"So, what happens now?"

"Now we get up, if we manage to find our legs—it seems I cannot feel mine and am not so certain they are still attached—and we return to our den to bathe. Within the next few days, I will attend Bafulk's hashavan. I will likely get notice of it within the next several days. Then, at the very next full moon here in about a week, we will be joined properly in a mating ceremony that my mother has been dreaming of for me since I was born," I say with a small laugh.

Kate burrows her face into my shoulder and groans.

"Okay, so I just have to survive whatever overdone thing your mother has imagined for us, and then we're free."

I nod, amused by the eagerness in her voice. I understand the feeling. I'm more than ready to finally be settled with my family with no more expectations or ceremonies. I drag my fingers across her skin as I speak. "Yes, for the most part. After our ceremony, we will be taking up our post among the orcs. We will be there for most of the year, but Mother will see to it that our den and territory are maintained."

Lifting her head, Kate smiles down at me. "I like this plan. You and me, Boukie and Cavekji doing what we're meant to do and being a family together. It's good."

I tickle her ribs to feel her squirm on top of me.

"Have you decided what you want to do now? Where your heart is?"

Kate pauses and licks her lips.

"I did have a thought, now that you mention it."

"And what is that, my love?"

A bright red flush steals over her face. "I'd like to study healing, if that's possible. Being with the females in the Warue territory… I felt really helpless, Cavek. I wanted to help them but couldn't do anything."

"You helped keep those kits alive."

She nods. "I did, because I was nursing Cavekji and produce an abundance. But I never want to feel that way again. I want to help people and be able to tend to any hurts my children suffer as they grow." She chews at her lip. "Do you think it's possible for a human to learn healing magic?"

I grin and kiss her soundly. "Don't be silly. Of course it is possible. Most of healing is relying on the spirits of the various herbs and your relationship with them. Hands-on energy manipulation, the kind that encourages a body to repair quicker, is something that all living beings can learn how to do. If this is what you feel your path is, I will proudly support it."

She shrieks with joy and presses against me, kissing me with renewed vigor. She's pouring all her love into me. I can feel it slide into me and that emptiness that I had never known I had inside before my Kate. Her hands begin to wander and this time she's the aggressor, and I love it. I arch my hips beneath her exploring hands and whisper out encouraging words.

We make love two more times at the lotus pond. Hard and fast, slow and sweet. We explore each other and revel in the way our bodies join, making us a singular whole being if only for a short time.

∼

Kate

When we're done making love, the flowers have closed their luminous buds and only the softest glow of the vines remains to light our way home. I look up at my mate as he draws me into our den and allow peace and happiness to flow freely within me.

Cavek is my wellspring of love that I thought I would never have. And our love is the foundation upon which I can, for the first time, build our future with complete trust. I kiss him, committed heart and soul.

EPILOGUE

TWO MONTHS LATER

KATE

We're settled in at our new home among the orcs. It's a charming little cottage in the heart of the village. Boukie loves it already. She misses Bafulk but is making new friends easily among the children in the village.

For our part, Cavek and I have been enjoying so much quality time together. He still has duties that take him out of our home, just as I do with my training as a healer, and there are obligations we fulfill as a couple, but it's a slow-paced life for the most part. The visits from dignitaries from other orc clans are probably among the more exciting things that happen around here.

The gathering of clans a few weeks ago ranked higher on the exciting scale than I really wanted to experience. Among one of the visiting clans, someone accidentally let loose a small pack of griffin hatchlings that he was transporting to the mountains to set free. Each about the size of a pit bull, they caused quite a bit of damage before the one responsible for their care rounded them up.

I started feeling sick within days of the last of the clans departing. I chalked it up to overexcitement and a bit of indigestion. But when I wasn't better after a few days, Cavek insisted that we go see the healer. Now that Cavek and I are seated in the healer's cottage, I'm certain it's something else.

The healer, Vashma, settles across from us, her heavy robes spilling around her. The entire sight is quite serene. I could appreciate it more if my heart wasn't trying to jump out of my throat.

"I doubt that you need me to tell you this, Kate, but from what I can tell you are in your early stages of pregnancy."

I can't even enjoy Cavek's look of shock.

"The High Sun Festival?" my mate in a small voice.

Vashma raises her brows and snorts.

"Pixie dust, of course. No wonder you're expecting. You have done this before, Kate, so you know to take it easy but don't worry about keeping to your regular routine. And congratulations, you two," she beams with pleasure. It's not often she consults on a pregnancy and she always enjoys giving the news.

Cavek swallows and a hint of panic comes over his features. With Cavekji still very much a baby and entering into his evil toddler period, neither one of us is prepared for another baby so close in age.

"Well, this is a bit unexpected," he manages to say.

I snort and pat my mate on the shoulder.

"Just you wait. You get to be there for it all this time. The mood swings, the hormones, and sleepless nights with a newborn," I chuckle with glee as he noticeably pales.

Oh, yes. He's in for a good time.

. . .

Seven years later
    Cavek

Our youngest, Bisak, giggles at me as he scrambles out of the tub and attempts to get away. He loves these games too much. At three years old, he's a tiny terror. Whenever we go back to the Middling Way, Serus keeps trying to hand him blunt weapons, such as staves and clubs, which I promptly have to take away before Kate sees. Trolls don't count these as proper weapons, but Kate doesn't agree. And after watching Bisak nearly clobber his brother with the last club, I'm starting to agree with her.

I loop an arm around the wriggling trollbie as he attempts to squirm out of my hold, his body still slick with soap and water. It's like holding onto a fish. With immense effort, I finally pull his sleeping tunic on him and set him on the floor so that I can stretch out my back. I only blink and my trollbie is back in the tub, this time fully clothed.

I growl at Bisak, and he responds with a cheerful grin so like his uncle it gives me pause and a touch of homesickness. I rub my hands over my face and scowl at my offspring.

"Look at this mess, Bisak. Now I have to get you back out and dry you *again*."

"Up. Up. Love you, Daddy," he chirps, his arms coming up in a show of cooperation.

With a muttered oath, I sweep him back up out of the water, strip off the soggy tunic, dry him for the second time, and pull a fresh one back over his head.

Hours later when both Kate and I are sitting in exhaustion by the fire, and our children are tucked in bed, I look over at her and rub my hand lovingly over hers. She's never looked more beautiful and precious to me. I doubt that even time will change that.

"I love you, mate. More than anything," I murmur.

She opens one eye and smiles at me. "I love you too, Cavek."

"Please don't take this the wrong way, but I think I have reached my limit for offspring."

She closes her eyes and groans.

"Thank the gods. You and me both."

Ten years later
Kate

Sammi and I share conspiring smiles as we watch our children flirt. Cavekji is courting with her second born, another daughter named Amvola. Ferona stands nearby making rude noises at them and laughing uproariously over it while her sister blushes angrily. My son is slow to anger. If not for the cheerful shade of mint green to his complexion, his disposition is so mellow that people often tell me that he doesn't seem like a troll, even a half-troll. Instead of taking offense at Ferona's antics, he rolls his eyes at his best friend and pulls Amvola to her feet so that they can find a more private place.

I still can't believe that Cavekji is formally courting my best friend's daughter. That's the dream of nearly every best friend, that their children might marry—or mate in this case.

Not that we're likely to get lucky again. Aside from her oldest two daughters, Sammi has a wild brood of boys. She and Orgath have been busy populating his clan almost single-handedly, whereas Cavek and I only had two more children after Cavekji and have taken a potion to null our fertility for many years so we can enjoy each other. Now that they're nearly all out of the den, I'm looking forward to some real alone time.

My tart-mouthed little apple-green daughter Melia sits a short distance away with a book. She wrinkles her nose at the whole thing. She's insisted quite firmly that she's not interested in finding a mate, although I've caught her casting looks of interest when Ferona's mate-to-be visits with his kin from a neighboring orc clan. At sixteen, she's still young and I, frankly, am not in *that* huge of a hurry for her to grow up. Cavek blames her mischievous nature on pixie magic from the night of her conception. I give her a pointed look to not torment her brother. She grins and concedes with a nod. Foiled again.

To my surprise, Boukie arrived this morning from the mountains where she lives with her mate, an ancient dragon with the most sarcastic temperament I've ever encountered. I thought dragons would be wise, not wise-asses, but I like him. Orgath and Cavek do as well. In the far field beyond the keep, they are sparring. The males insist they aren't too old for such things, although Sammi and I often exchange dubious looks over the matter.

Sundays have become a sort of unofficial family day, to the point that they've taken over the Sunday dinner traditions we had back home in Ov'Ge.

At my side, Sammi stands up from her seat and taunts her boys at the top of her lungs. Bisak, now thirteen, scampers around the older boys like an excited puppy. Just behind him, one of Stitch's pups from last season's litter races after him, its tail wagging. Sammi's teasing hits home. In response, all the boys—even Bisak—bellow and throw themselves into trying to conquer "the enemy" also known as their fathers.

Sammi raises her glass to me in a lighthearted toast.

"To us."

"To love," I rejoin.

"To family," Boukie says as she watches the boys. "The odd group that we are."

I laugh and agree that I can drink to that. Nearby, Cavek waves to me and I blow him a kiss.

Tonight, I mouth to my mate. He winks at me, and the boyish grin that spreads across his handsome face sets my heart racing.

Even after all these years, it takes so little effort on his part. His hair has faded into the palest purple hue and the grooves on his face from his time with the werewolves have deepened some, but not as much as the laughter lines around his mouth and eyes from our years of happiness together. I have no shortage of gray hairs myself and a few modest wrinkles, but Cavek makes me feel cherished like I'm still the most beautiful woman for him.

I smile and sip my drink, counting the hours until I will get my mate alone again.

AUTHOR'S NOTE

I hope you enjoyed Kate and Cavek's story. When I wrote the Orc Wife, I knew immediately that I wanted to go back and tell their story, just because they are such a fun couple and quite different from Sammi and Orgath. It of course presented a few unique challenges, one of which was how to tell their story without literally rehashing the entire third of the Orc Wife. While writing this I really began to love the characters, especially Boukie.

Of course, everyone always wants to know what characters are getting stories so I will go on record to say at this point the characters that have made an appearance that are definitely getting slotted for stories are Bodi (with a reappearance of his brother Farli and Jason), Serus later this fall in the Troll King, and Boukie with her Dragon this winter. I also have the Accidental Werewolf's Mate, Unicorn's Mare and the Pixie Queen that will be coming out this year. A lot is on its way for the Monstery Yours series!

The next book coming out is The Accidental Werewolf's Mate. A drunken encounter between a human woman and an Evarue werewolf inadvertently leads to an unintentional mating

AUTHOR'S NOTE

bite and now they have to see just how they are going to make the whole mate thing work.

As always you can follow me (SJ Sanders) on Facebook and join my group Mate Index Sweethearts. Also, if you are looking for merchandise, check out my shop: https://www.zazzle.com/store/sexybeastdesigns

S.J. Sanders

Printed in Great Britain
by Amazon